Robert J. Harris

Kelpies is an imprint of Floris Books

First published in 2014 by Floris Books
© 2014 Robert J. Harris
Second printing 2015

The publisher acknowledges subsidy from
Creative Scotland towards the publication
of this volume

This book is also
available as an eBook

British Library CIP data available
ISBN 978-178250-122-0
Printed & Bound by MBM Print SCS Ltd, Glasgow

To my friend Jane Yolen,
who made me be a writer.
Thanks, Jane!

1. WHO IS LARRY O'KEEFE?

It was the third day of a heatwave that had Scotland baking like pancakes on a griddle. Old people were advised to stay indoors, everybody smelled of sun block, and there were warnings all over telling you not to leave your dog in the car.

Lewis McBride was seated on a folding chair in the back garden reading a detective novel about a scientist who tracked down a murderer by using a neutrino detector. Lewis had calculated that fifteen minutes in the sun was enough to soak up a healthy dose of vitamin D without risking sunburn, and he had decided to take it early in the morning before the heat became too intense.

He was just finishing the final chapter of the story when his watch beeped three times to indicate the fifteen minutes was up. As if on cue, the kitchen door burst open and Lewis' brother barged into the back garden, shattering the peace. At fourteen, Greg was a year older than Lewis, but Lewis had always considered himself to be the mature one.

Greg was dressed in baggy shorts, flip-flops and sunglasses. In one hand he was swinging a bag full of empty cola cans that jangled noisily. Cradled in his other arm was an enormous water gun called a Splazooka that he had bought last summer. The day after he bought the Splazooka it rained and went on raining for three weeks. The Splazooka had been hibernating in Greg's cupboard ever since.

Whistling the theme tune from *Match Of The Day*, Greg took out the cans he'd retrieved from the recycling bin and set them up in a line across the picnic table at the back of the garden.

"What are you doing?" Lewis asked.

"Target practice," Greg answered, setting down the last of the cans. He took six paces back and started making adjustments to the Splazooka. Lewis noted that his brother had added extra tubing and some springs.

"Your water gun looks different," he observed.

"That's right," said Greg. "I've cranked it up to double its firepower."

"What do you want to do that for?"

"Because EU regulations stop them making it as strong as it could be."

"What are you talking about?"

"It stands to reason, doesn't it? The government

needs water cannons to stop riots and stuff, so they can't have people shooting back with things that are just as powerful."

"So you've given it a boost?" said Lewis dubiously.

"Sure," Greg said. "It's just a matter of hydraulics." He turned the gun in Lewis' direction. "Here, do you fancy a blast? It'll cool you off." He placed a finger on the trigger.

"No!" yelled Lewis. "This is a library book!" He hid the book behind his back and threw a protective arm up in front of his face.

Just then there came a loud whoop from behind the hedge. The back gate flew open and Susie Spinetti burst into the garden.

Greg promptly shot a stream of water in her direction. Susie ducked under it nimbly and poked him hard in the stomach as she darted past.

Greg doubled over. "Oof! Not so rough, Spinny!"

"Aw, Greg, you can take it. Did you not eat your porridge this morning?"

"I'm a chocolate nut flakes man."

"No wonder you're so slow, eating that muck."

Susie was dressed in shorts and a Fife Flames T-shirt, with a rainbow-coloured headband around her short black hair. At school Susie was captain of the girls' football team, champion of her year in running and javelin, and was a top scorer for Fife's junior ice hockey team, the Flames. She often burst in on the McBrides at the end of her morning jog.

"It's a gorgeous day, Greg!" she enthused. "How about a dip in the Castle Rock Pool?"

Still rubbing his stomach, Greg gave her a disgruntled look. "You should watch yourself, Spinny. They used to drown witches there, you know."

"I'll take my chances. So, how about it?"

"It's too hot to go swimming. If you want to cool off, I've got just the thing."

He aimed the Splazooka at her again. Susie stepped forward and plugged the nozzle with her finger. "Careful, Greg," she told him. "If you press the trigger now, it'll blow up right in your face."

Greg pulled the water gun away. "It would be just like you to break it, right when we've finally got the weather for a water fight."

Susie rolled her eyes. "Stop worrying about your toys, Greg. How about we go skating at the Kirkcaldy ice rink?"

"Can you not see I'm busy? Maybe tomorrow."

"Tomorrow I'm off to hockey camp for a week. Got to work on my slap shot." She swung an imaginary hockey stick with such ferocity Lewis jerked back as if she'd fired a puck straight at him.

"You dragged me off to play tennis yesterday," said Greg, "and before that it was cycling out to Tentsmuir. Could we not take a break?"

Susie put her hands on her hips. "Greg, you're not being much of a boyfriend."

Greg scowled back at her. "Spinny, I am *not* your boyfriend."

"Of course you are, Greg. You've even come up with a cute nickname for me."

It's not cute. It's supposed to be offensive."

Susie hiccuped with laughter and gave him a playful punch in the arm. "Oh, Greg, you're so funny. The things you *say*!"

Lewis decided it was time to intervene. "I see you've got new trainers, Susie," he observed.

"Well spotted, that boy," said Susie, hoisting her leg up at an impossible angle so that her foot was right in front of Lewis' face. "They're Skyliners, the Rolls Royce of sporting footwear. My dad's just got a load of them in for the shop."

Susie's family owned a sporting goods store, so she always had access to the latest equipment.

Lewis gently pushed her foot back down. "I'm going inside now, before I turn into a lobster."

"Lewis, you've only been out here five minutes!" Greg said scornfully.

Lewis ignored him and headed into the kitchen. Susie followed him inside. "I'm parched," she said, clutching her throat. "Have you got anything to drink in here?"

Before Lewis could respond, she flung open the fridge and helped herself to a carton of cold orange juice. From outside came the sound of cans being shot off the table and bouncing off the back fence.

Lewis' dad came in from the other side of the house, waving a copy of the local paper. "Fame at last," he declared. "I expect Hollywood will be on the phone any time now."

"Dad, have you been out in the sun too long?" asked Lewis.

His dad folded the paper open and displayed it. "Look at this picture here."

It was a large colour photograph of a group of golfers on St Andrews' Old Course. Mr McBride was in the middle of them. Since he was the golf course manager there was nothing unusual about that. What made it newsworthy was the figure standing right beside him, smiling brightly enough to shatter the camera lens.

Susie craned over Lewis' shoulder. "Hey!" she exclaimed excitedly. "Isn't that Garth Makepeace?"

"That's right," said Lewis' dad, "the big film star. He was after my autograph, of course, but I wouldn't give it to him."

Susie laughed through a gurgle of juice. "Mr Mac, you crack me up."

Lewis was still studying the photo. In his last action blockbuster, Garth Makepeace had played the part of a brave explorer in search of a lost city deep in the Amazon jungle. Lewis was surprised to see that in real life the actor was hardly any taller than his father.

"That's funny," he said. "In his films he looks nearly seven feet tall."

"Nice chap though," said his dad. "Bought us all lunch after the game."

There were half a dozen other men in the picture, all prominent members of the St Andrews business community, but as Lewis' eyes drifted along the line, he almost choked.

The man on the far right was smiling just as much as Garth Makepeace, but there was a nasty edge to his smile, like somebody who's left a family of frogs in your bed after stealing your valuables. He had red hair, a lean, wily face, and a small, tapered beard. It was a face Lewis knew only too well, one he never expected to see again.

He grabbed the paper so abruptly his dad almost jumped out of his skin.

"Lewis!" his dad gasped.

Lewis was out the back door. He seized Greg by

the shoulder and spun him round to face him. "Look at this!"

Greg gave the picture the barest glance and went back to his target practice. "Sure, Dad's in the paper again. Big deal." He blasted a can off the table and yelled, "Bullseye!"

"Look who else is there," Lewis insisted. He shoved the paper under his brother's nose and pointed out the red-haired man.

Greg whipped off his sunglasses for a closer look and jumped back with a yelp. "Are you kidding me?" His finger tightened reflexively on the trigger of the Splazooka and Lewis took the full force of the jet right in the face.

"Watch where you're pointing that thing!" he spluttered, shoving the gun barrel aside.

Greg pocketed his sunglasses and dropped the water gun. "Loki!" he said, snatching the paper and glaring at it. "What's Dad doing hanging around with that creep?"

Months ago, Lewis and Greg had accidentally cast a magic spell that restored a long-lost eighth day of the week, Lokiday, the day belonging to Loki, the god of magic and mischief. The effect was to turn St Andrews into a mad fantasy world filled with ogres and goblins, ruled over by Loki himself. The boys had only just managed to reverse the spell and send him back where he came from.

The brothers charged into the kitchen where Susie had polished off the orange juice and was helping herself to a banana. "Greg, did you see your dad's palling around with Garth Makepeace?"

"I see who he's palling around with," Greg retorted. "Dad, who is this guy?" He pointed at the picture. "The one with the beard."

"Him? Let me think." Mr McBride tapped his moustache as though checking it was still there. "Larry, he said his name was. Larry O'Keefe."

"Larry O'Keefe," Lewis repeated. "And who is he, exactly?"

Dad thought for a moment. "Some sort of businessman. Flew in from America a couple of days ago. He's staying at the Old Course Hotel. I think he said he owned a string of joke shops."

"That figures," said Lewis.

Greg tossed the paper onto the table and he and Lewis went into a huddle by the microwave.

"What do you think he's up to?" Lewis said in an anxious whisper. "I thought we'd seen the last of him."

Greg screwed up his face in thought. "Remember the other gods took away his powers when they banned Lokiday, his special day? He told us he was living as a gambler in America, so how much trouble can he be?"

"Hey, did you guys get air conditioning or

something?" asked Susie. "It's turned awful cold all of a sudden."

Lewis and Greg looked round and saw her rubbing her bare arms.

"She's right, you know," said their dad. "It has turned chilly."

Lewis glanced out the back window and groaned. "No wonder. Look outside!"

The sky, which had been a brilliant blue a minute before, was now covered in dark clouds, and thick snowflakes were falling on the garden.

"That's queer," said their dad. "Snow in the middle of July. What could have brought that on?"

Lewis and Greg looked at each other. "Loki!" they both declared at once.

2. A BOX FULL OF WINTER

"What was that, boys?" said Mr McBride.

"Just saying 'look', Dad," said Lewis, covering quickly. "You know, at the snow."

No one but the boys themselves remembered anything about the spell Loki had cast on the town before. There was no way to explain it that would be believable.

"Here comes Mum," said Greg.

Mrs McBride had just pulled up in the car at the back of the house. She was dressed in a short sleeved blouse and a summer skirt, and hurried into the house, shivering. She dropped two bags of groceries on the kitchen table and shook the snow out of her hair.

"Who broke the weather?" she asked. "When I went off to the shops it was like the Bahamas out there. I nearly froze to death on the way back."

"It must be some unusual climatic thing," said Mr McBride, flicking the switch on the central heating. "A funnel of cold air coming in from Iceland or something like that."

"That weather girl on the BBC didn't say anything about this," said Mum. "You'd think she'd know her business, being Scottish."

"It's going to play havoc with the course," said Mr McBride. "I'd better get on to the groundskeepers." He pulled out his phone and disappeared into the study.

"If this keeps up, the car's going to get buried," said Lewis, glancing out the window.

"I'd put it away in the garage, if there was any room," said Mum, sorting through the shopping, "but it's full of junk. I keep asking your dad to clear it out."

"Is this freaky or what?" said Susie, bouncing on the spot to keep herself from freezing. "No trips to the beach today."

"And I was planning to visit the Botanic Gardens too," said Mum, "to see their new orchids." She finished stacking some tins on a shelf. "Susie, I'd better loan you a coat and give you a lift home."

"It's only a couple of streets, Mrs Mac," said Susie. "I'll just run and wrap up warm when I get there. I'll see you boys outside for a snowball fight," she added as she jogged out the door. "Better watch your backs!"

"I think we'd all better get some warm clothes on," said Mum, "before somebody catches a chill."

Lewis and Greg went upstairs to change out of their ␣␣␣er clothes into jeans, jumpers and winter socks.

They met up again in Lewis' room and stared out the window at the impossible snow.

"Be straight with me, Lewis," said Greg. "You haven't been messing around with any old books or reading out magical rhymes, have you?"

It was an ancient rhyme in an old book Lewis had found that had enchanted the town and summoned Loki a few months ago.

"Do you think I'm off my head?" retorted Lewis. "And can I just say that last time it was your idea to say the rhyme that brought Loki here."

"There's no point dwelling on the past," said Greg, waving a dismissive hand. "We need to focus on the here and now. Look, at least nothing's happened to change the town."

"No, but this freak weather and Loki turning up at the same time – it can't be a coincidence."

"Last time we saw him he had the power to conjure up fire," Greg recalled, "but that was only because he'd brought his special day, Lokiday, back from the past. Without that he can't do magic any more than we could."

"Something different is happening this time," said Lewis. "And I'm sure it will get worse."

"Then we'd better get busy, Lewis," Greg declared. "We need to find this Larry O'Keefe and shut him down."

"Last time he nearly roasted us alive," Lewis pointed out with a worried frown.

"Yes, but without his powers he's just a conman in a fancy suit. We can take him."

"I don't suppose we have a choice. It's not like anybody would believe us if we told them."

"Too right," said Greg. "I don't see the police arresting him for causing magical mayhem just on our say so."

Lewis peered out the window. The snow was still falling, if anything, even heavier, it seemed to him. He shivered. "We'd better dig out our winter gear."

They put on their woolly hats, coats and heavy boots and headed downstairs. Mum had the TV on in the front room and they could hear the voice of a news reporter.

"The Met Office is baffled by the freak snowfall in St Andrews. While the wintry conditions are limited to this one area, they show no sign of easing."

Dad came out of the study, still with his phone in his hand. "This blizzard is messing up the signal," he said. "Where are you two going? Off to do a bit of sledging, I suppose."

"That's right, Dad, we're taking the sledge over to Hallowhill," said Greg.

"You have fun," said Dad, poking at his phone. "If ˉ can't get through to the clubhouse, I'll have to drive there in person."

"Dad can you tell us anything more about Larry O'Keefe?" Lewis asked.

"I'm afraid I don't follow you, son."

"I mean, did he do or say anything strange or unusual?"

"Well, he slices the ball something awful, I can tell you that. He was only part of the group because he'd met Garth Makepeace on the flight over."

"He was with Garth Makepeace?" blurted Greg.

"Garth – he said to call him Garth – had a round booked on the Old Course and he invited Larry along," Dad explained. "But anybody with eyes could see Larry wasn't much of a golfer."

"How's that, Dad?"

"Well, he lost a ball in the burn under the Swilken Bridge."

"What's the Swilken Bridge?" asked Lewis.

Greg shook his head despairingly. "Even you should know that, Lewis! It's only one of the most famous landmarks on the course."

"It crosses the burn between the first and eighteenth greens," said Dad. "It's been there for 700 years."

"What about Larry O'Keefe, Dad?" Lewis persisted.

Dad looked amused. "Right. He plopped a ball into the burn right under the bridge. He spent ten minutes splashing about under there. Lost the ball completely, but came out with a box he'd found. The funny thing was, he seemed pretty pleased with himself."

Dad went back to his phone as the boys stepped outside. The neighbouring gardens and the street were covered over with a thick layer of white, like icing on a Christmas cake. A car crawled past, leaving a set of tyre tracks in its wake. Even as they watched, the falling snow began filling in the furrows.

As they started down the Canongate Road, Greg said, "Do you have to wear that duffel coat? You look like Paddington Bear."

"I do not!" Lewis retorted. "Plus it's really warm, I'll have you know."

Before Greg could open his mouth again a snowball thumped into his back. "She shoots, she scores!" called a familiar voice.

Another snowball caught Lewis in the shoulder as they turned around.

There stood Susie, dressed in her winter gear, leaning on her ice hockey stick. She laughed and scooped up another handful of snow. Lewis dodged as the snowball went whizzing past his ear.

"Spinny, are you just looking for trouble?" Greg asked.

"I told you I'd see you outside for a snowball fight. vou listen to anything?"

"Why have you got your hockey stick?" asked Lewis.

"Because it's dead brilliant for skiting snow about," Susie told him. "See?"

Bounding forward, she took a savage swing and smacked a heap of snow right in their faces. Lewis squawked and stumbled back, wiping his eyes with the back of his glove.

Greg scooped up a double handful of snow and pressed it into a ball. "You asked for it, Spinny!" he said, letting fly.

With a casual flick of her hockey stick, Susie smashed the snowball to bits in mid-air. "Some technique, eh?" she grinned.

"That's great, Susie," said Lewis, "but we don't have time for this right now." He grabbed hold of Greg's arm to keep him from making another snowball.

Greg recovered himself and pulled his arm away. "He's right. We're busy."

"Busy?" said Susie. "How can you be busy on a snow day? I'll bet half the town's shut down already."

"We've got to go and find Larry O'Keefe," said Greg.

"What for? Who is this Larry O'Keefe anyway?"

"Nobody," said Lewis. "We're just running an errand for Dad. Aren't we, Greg?"

"Uh huh," Greg agreed.

Susie gave them a hard stare. "Look, this snow is

obviously a freak thing and it probably won't last long," she said, drumming her fingers on her hockey stick. "We should make the most of it."

Greg began edging away. "Tomorrow we'll go diving or camel riding or whatever you want. Promise."

"I told you I'm going to hockey camp tomorrow," Susie reminded him sharply.

"Then you'd better go home and pack."

The brothers made off in the direction of town. Lewis braced his shoulders, half expecting to get a snowball in the neck, but nothing happened. When he judged they were safely out of range, he turned to his brother. "You like her, don't you?"

Greg glanced back to make sure Susie wasn't following. "She's okay," he said with a shrug.

"No," said Lewis, "I mean you like her, like a girlfriend."

"She is not my girlfriend. It's Susie. We pal around together, that's all."

"Suit yourself."

"You're just saying that because you've been pining over Lindsay Jensen ever since her family moved to Aberdeen," snorted Greg.

Lewis reddened. "I have not."

"Right, then it's settled," said Greg. "You're not and Susie is just a pal."

"Fine," said Lewis, "she's a pal." And let the subject drop.

Blanketed with snow, Bridge Street looked like a ski slope. As the brothers climbed the hill, they had to dodge some kids who were sledging down in the opposite direction. At the bus station on City Road they saw the Dundee bus was stuck in the snow. A group of shivering passengers had got out and were struggling to push it free.

As he thought nervously about facing the enemy who had almost destroyed them once before, Lewis couldn't help wishing he was a little more like Greg. What was the right word for it? Simple minded? That sounded a bit harsh. But things always looked simple to Greg. He didn't study up or calculate the odds, he just charged in. And if he banged his head or tripped over, he shook it off and kept on going.

Lewis, by contrast, was too aware of how complicated everything was, geometry, the economy, growing up. He was already trying to work out which school subjects would give him the best chance of making it to university and finding a job. Greg acted as if all he had to do was come up with some kind of trick and everything would fall into his lap, as if by magic.

And here he was now, leading them off to confront a Norse god as if it were no more dangerous than a trip to the shops.

A short trudge brought them to a mini-roundabout marking the entrance to the Old Course Hotel. As they started down the drive, the pair of them saw something that made them stop dead in their tracks.

To their left lay the deserted playing fields of Station Park. To their right lay an empty car park. Dead ahead a familiar red-bearded figure was striding energetically towards them as if the flurrying snow didn't bother him in the least.

He was wearing a long fur coat and a fedora. As he drew closer, they could see his green eyes flashing beneath the brim of his hat.

Loki.

The Norse god stopped short at the sight of them and grimaced. "You two? I'm beginning to think you've nothing better to do with your time than get under my feet. Shouldn't you be in school?"

"It's the summer holiday," said Lewis.

"And you're ruining it with this blizzard of yours," Greg added boldly.

"What makes you think I had anything to do with it?" Loki asked innocently.

"It's just the sort of thing you'd do," said Greg. "Because you're such a creep."

"Yes, you know me too well," Loki agreed ruefully. "But how did you know where to find me?"

"If you want privacy," Greg informed him, "you shouldn't get your picture in the paper."

"It was vanity, I suppose," Loki admitted, stroking his beard. "I couldn't say no to being photographed with a movie star."

"And why are you calling yourself Larry O'Keefe now?" asked Lewis.

Loki waved the question away with an airy hand. "Kid, I change my name more often than you change your underwear. It's all part of being a professional trickster."

"But you don't have magic powers any more," said Lewis. "You told us that last time we met."

"So how are you pulling this off?" Greg demanded.

"Because I have this," said Loki.

With a flourish he pulled a wooden box out of his pocket. It was about the size of a small box of chocolates and Lewis could see that its surface was carved with runes, the writing of the ancient Norse peoples.

"This box was manufactured for me centuries ago by the Troll King," Loki explained smugly. "It contains the Fimbulwinter. That is to say, it did until I opened the lid and let it out."

"The Fimbulwinter," said Lewis. "I read about that in Myths of the Vikings. It's supposed to be one of the signs of the end of the world, what the Vikings called Ragnarok."

"Been boning up on your Norse legends, eh?" said Loki with a wicked smile. "Not that it will help you."

"Lewis, how is it you know all that stuff," said Greg, "but you've never heard of the Swilken Bridge?"

"I'm just not interested in sports," Lewis retorted. "That's not a crime, is it?"

"So, Larry," said Greg, turning his attention back to Loki, "last time it was a book, this time it's a box. What's next? A magic toothbrush?"

"There isn't going to be a next time," said Loki, baring his teeth. "This time I'm playing for keeps."

"It looks to me like you're planning to open a ski resort," said Greg.

"Mostly the snow is to keep people off the streets so they don't get in my way," said Loki, "but in your case it's obviously going to take a little more than that." His smile widened nastily. "You see, as long as I possess the box, I control all this snow."

He gripped the box tightly in one hand while with the other he made a magical gesture. The snow at his feet rippled and heaved. As Greg and Lewis watched in amazement, it formed a conical mound eight feet high. The mound sprouted a bulbous head and a set of stumpy arms. Then, with a ponderous shudder, it lurched forward on a pair of legs as thick as post-boxes.

Lewis took a step back. "We'd better get out of here."

"Relax, Lewis, it's only a snowman," said Greg. "A few good kicks will knock it to bits."

Even as he spoke, the lumpy snow creature hardened into a glittering statue of clear greenish ice. Its face became a crystal mask of jutting angles. Claws like icicles bristled from its hands.

Lewis gulped. "I think it's a lot worse than a snowman."

"Actually it's more of an ice monster," said Loki. "Here, why don't you get acquainted?"

He waved the creature forward and it stomped towards the boys, slashing the air with its jagged claws.

"Run!" yelled Lewis.

The brothers wheeled around and bolted. Almost at once they found themselves floundering in the snow. The monster came after them with a noise like icebergs colliding.

Bounding clumsily from drift to drift, the boys fled along Station Road.

Lewis could hear the creature's icy talons clashing behind him like steel shears. Straining for speed, he slipped and sprawled flat on his face.

Greg seized his elbow and tried to haul him up.

"Come on, Lewis, move!" he urged. He lost his footing and flopped down right beside his brother.

His heart pounding, Lewis looked up and saw Loki's monster looming over them. It raised its claws and prepared to strike.

3. A MAN CALLED MALLET

Lewis gritted his teeth and braced himself for the deadly blow.

But at that instant a figure leaped suddenly from the narrow alleyway of Granny Clarke's Wynd, like a rabbit popping out of its hole.

It was Susie Spinetti.

As the monster lunged at the boys, she swung her hockey stick and hooked it around its ankle. The boys rolled desperately aside as the ice creature toppled face first into the snow.

"Ka-BOOM!" Susie crowed in triumph.

It was what she shouted whenever she scored a goal.

"Spinny!" Greg exclaimed, as he struggled to his feet, pulling Lewis up beside him.

"Come on, you two, don't hang about!" Susie cried, bounding off in her thick-soled boots. "Good thing for you I hung back in defence."

"It's lucky for us she's a pal," said Lewis, as he and Greg toiled after her.

The deep snow made it impossible to move quickly. When Lewis glanced back he saw the ice monster heave itself upright. With a noise like an avalanche, it started after them, closing the gap with long, purposeful strides.

"We'll never get away from that thing!" Lewis gasped.

"We'll have to stand and fight then," said Greg. "Here, give me a loan of that stick, Spinny."

"Don't be daft," said Susie. "Come on, we'll duck in here."

She swerved left, vaulted up a couple of steps and dived through the revolving door of the Rannoch Hotel. The boys dashed in behind her and stumbled into the brightly lit foyer.

Following hard on their heels, the snow monster hurled itself at the revolving door. Without a brain to understand how the door worked, the creature got trapped in one section. Instead of exiting, it sent the door into a wild spin.

Faster and faster it flew around, the monster clattering about like a glass tumbler in a washing machine. Chips flew off at every impact until suddenly it shattered into smithereens. When the door slowed to halt all that was left was a harmless scattering of ice.

"Fife Flames one, ice robots nil!" Susie declared with satisfaction.

Lewis yanked off his woolly hat. "Loki could easily whip up another one of those things to send after us," he muttered to Greg.

"The heat in here would probably melt it," said Greg.

"Fair enough," Lewis conceded, "but we can't stay put forever. Suppose Loki's waiting outside?"

"One thing at a time," said Greg, turning to Susie. "Not that we don't appreciate the help, Spinny, but what exactly are you doing here?"

"I knew you were up to something," said Susie, "and it's easy to trail folk when they leave footprints in the snow." She fixed them with a challenging stare. "If you ask me, it's you boys that have got some explaining to do."

Lewis noticed that they were drawing disapproving glances from a number of guests who were seated in comfy chairs sipping coffee.

"Over here," he said, leading the way to a quiet spot by a potted rubber plant.

Susie lost no time in getting to the point. "Spill it. Who is that guy in the fur coat and how did he make that monster come out of the snow?"

As Lewis groped for words, the revolving door spun around and Loki came sauntering across the hotel lobby. He scanned the foyer and Lewis' heart skipped a beat when his sharp eyes spotted them.

Loki popped a stick of chewing gum into his mouth and walked over to them.

"No cigar today?" Greg inquired.

"My doctor told me to give them up," said Loki.

Lewis forced himself to speak boldly. "That's right, without any magic powers, you're just a guy."

"And you can't pull any of your snow tricks in here," said Greg.

"Don't be so sure of that," said Loki. He raised an eyebrow at Susie. "And who's this little spitfire?"

"Leave her out of it," said Greg, stepping between them.

Loki removed his hat and scratched his head. "Take it from me, toots," he told Susie, "hanging around with these chuckleheads will only buy you trouble."

"Toots?" Susie echoed indignantly. "Who do you think you're talking to?"

Ignoring her, Loki addressed the boys. "Last time we met up you got lucky, plain and simple. But if you cross me again, it will take more than a trick door to save you." He put his hat back on and headed to the exit. "Take a telling and back off."

As he disappeared through the revolving door, Lewis let out the breath he had been holding. "I thought he might whip up another blizzard right here," he said.

"He was bluffing," Greg snorted.

"Did you hear what he called me? Toots!" Susie exclaimed, as though that were all that mattered. She took an angry step towards the door. "I've half a mind to go after him and—"

"That's a bad idea," said Lewis, blocking her way.

Susie eyed him crossly, then turned to Greg. "I'm still waiting for an explanation from you two," she said, bouncing the blade of her hockey stick off the palm of one hand. "And it better be good."

Greg rubbed his jaw. "Well, since you've jumped right into the middle of things, I suppose you might as well know the whole story."

He and Lewis took turns telling, as briefly as possible, how Loki had conjured up a magical day that transformed the whole of St Andrews and how they had only just been able to turn everything back to normal. It had happened months ago and they definitely hadn't expected to see him again.

There was a long silence while Susie stared at them. "Okay," she said at last, "who is he really?"

"We just told you," said Greg.

Susie clucked her tongue. "Greg, I wasn't born yesterday. I don't believe in Norse gods and magic and stuff any more than I believe in ghosts or fairies. Come on, what is he? A space alien?"

Lewis knew there was never any point arguing with

Susie. "All right, you guessed it," he said. "He's a space alien."

"From Planet X or something," Greg agreed.

Susie grinned. "Well, why didn't you just say so in the first place?" She gave her hockey stick a warlike shake. "We'll teach him to invade *our* planet!"

Just then a young woman in a smart uniform approached them from the reception desk. "Excuse me, can I help you?" she asked primly. "I don't think you're guests here." She cast a wary eye over Susie's hockey stick.

Before Lewis could say they were just sheltering from the blizzard, Greg declared loudly, "We're here for the spoons."

The woman raised her eyebrows. "Spoons?"

"Right. We're collecting spoons for charity. To help starving people in Burpovia."

Lewis groaned, but there was no stopping Greg now.

"Are people starving in – what was it? – *Burpovia?*" the woman inquired.

"You bet they are," said Greg. "We're collecting spoons, selling them, and using the money to send food to Burpovia. So how about it? Have you got any spare spoons?"

The woman peered at him for a few seconds then said, "I don't think so. We need all our spoons for our guests."

"Fine. If you're going to be miserly about it, we'll be off," said Greg.

He gestured to the other two and marched off towards the rear of the hotel. "Did you see that?" he said when Lewis and Susie caught up. "She couldn't have cared less about the people in Burpovia."

"There's no such place," Lewis objected.

"Of course there is," said Greg. "You should pay more attention in geography."

Susie chuckled. "Oh, Greg, the things you *say*."

Lewis shook his head. "Where are we going?"

"Do you not remember when Dad took us all here for lunch? There's a back door we can use. Just in case Loki has a snowman hanging about out front."

As they emerged from the back of the hotel they faced the full blast of the icy wind sweeping across the golf course from the sea.

"See, there's the Swilken Bridge there," said Greg pointing a gloved finger. The bridge was just an arch of snow now surrounded by more snow.

"That's where Dad says Loki found his magic box," said Lewis. "But what was it doing there in the first place?"

"Beats me," said Greg, striking out past a row of golf shops.

Lewis and Susie fell in behind him. "Should we not

call the government or the army?" asked Susie as they turned the corner into North Street.

"And tell them what?" said Greg. "That there are gods or aliens or monsters on the streets of St Andrews and they're the ones that are making it snow?"

"I see your point," said Susie. "It's at times like this you wish you had Dr Who's phone number."

"If only we knew what Loki was up to," said Lewis.

"Last time he was here he was pretty much trying to take over the world," Greg recalled.

"That's standard for aliens, taking over the world," said Susie grimly. "Their own planet's always dying or something."

"We need to come up with a plan," said Greg.

"That's going to be hard seeing as we've no idea what we're doing," said Lewis.

"That's the point, Lewis. Once we have a plan we'll know what we're doing. Try to be positive."

Lewis frowned in thought. "Well, I suppose, once we get home I could look through those books of Norse mythology I've got. And maybe we can find out something about Larry O'Keefe on the internet."

"Now you're thinking like a boss," Greg complimented him. "I'll see if I can rig up a flamethrower to take care of any ice monsters."

"A flamethrower?" said Susie sceptically. "Greg, you

nearly blew yourself up fiddling with your mum's coffee maker."

"This is different," said Greg. "I'm in war mode now."

"Maybe we can shelve the flamethrower until things get desperate," suggested Lewis.

"At this rate," said Susie, slogging through the snow, "it's going to take us all day to get back to your place."

"You're right," Lewis agreed. "This is a nightmare. And it doesn't seem to slow Loki down at all."

"He probably comes from an ice planet," said Susie. "That would explain a lot."

She broke off short as up ahead a pair of headlights stabbed through the gloom and a 4x4 Land Rover came into view.

"That's my dad!" exclaimed Susie. She waved her hockey stick over her head and yelled, "Hey, Dad! Over here!"

The vehicle pulled up and the passenger door swung open. Susie dived into the front and the boys got in back. Mr Spinetti had the heater on and it was a relief to be in the warm.

"What are you doing here?" Susie asked.

"Looking for you," answered Mr Spinetti as the car started moving again. "We tried phoning but the network's all messed up."

Greg slipped out his phone and confirmed that it wasn't working.

"You were supposed to be chucking snowballs around on Bannock Street," Mr Spinetti continued. "What are you doing down here?"

"We got carried away," said Susie. "You know what it's like."

"I don't mind losing my kids in the Amazon jungle," said Mr Spinetti, shifting gears, "but losing them in St Andrews would be embarrassing."

Susie chortled. "You'll not lose me that easy, Dad."

"This weather is ludicrous," said Mr Spinetti. "Most of the roads out of St Andrews are blocked already."

"I suppose hockey camp will be cancelled," said Susie glumly.

"Keep your fingers crossed," said her dad. "Maybe it'll all clear up by tomorrow."

They passed a council snowplough, its yellow lights flashing as it struggled through the drifts. Nearby, some hardy soul was trying to clear his path with a shovel. When they pulled up in front of the McBride house in Bannock Street, the boys saw there was a layer of snow a foot deep on the roof and the windows glinted with frost. Because it was so dark outside, all the lights were switched on.

"Thanks for the ride, Mr Spinetti," said Lewis and Greg as they climbed out.

Susie threw open her door as well. "I'll stay here with the boys," she said. "We could get back to our game of Star Blaster 3."

"I told your mum I'd bring you home," said Mr Spinetti.

"You don't want me sitting around our house being bored, do you?" Susie challenged him.

Lewis saw the side of her dad's mouth twitch as though at an unpleasant memory. "No, I definitely don't want that. You'll stay put at the McBrides' though?"

"Where else can I go in this?" said Susie, gesturing at the weather.

Inside, the heating was on full blast and it was as warm as toast. They all stripped off their coats and hats and trooped up to Lewis' room.

"I'll handle the online search," said Susie, plonking herself down at the desk. There was a bar of chocolate next to the mouse mat. She pounced on it and wolfed it down while the computer started up.

Greg stood over her, watching the screen. "You might have shared that," he complained.

"Too slow, Greg, too slow." Susie grabbed the mouse and clicked on an icon. She clicked again and again then shoved the mouse aside with a grunt. "It's no use. Your broadband's down."

She swivelled the chair round to face Lewis, who was sitting on the bed leafing through a book of Norse legends.

"You're wasting your time with those fairy stories," she told him.

"There's a lot of truth in these old myths," Lewis insisted, without looking up.

"He's right," Greg agreed. "We've seen it with our own eyes."

"Honestly, you two are that gullible," scoffed Susie. "I mean, ask yourselves which is more likely: that this guy with the ginger beard is a magical god from some ancient fantasy land or that he's an alien using a superior technology? Like when they ran into Apollo on that episode of Star Trek."

"At the end of the day, it doesn't make much difference," said Greg. "We need to get an edge. Let's go talk to Dad again. Maybe Loki let something slip while they were playing golf."

Downstairs, they found Mum in the living room watching the news.

"The BBC news is the only channel that's not breaking up," she said. "It looks like I'm going to miss tonight's episode of *The Inspector Golightly Mysteries*."

On the TV a reporter was talking to the camera. The caption below said he was in Strathkinness, just outside St Andrews. Behind him was a swirling cloud of white where St Andrews should have been.

"All roads in and out of the town are now completely blocked," the reporter said, "and all efforts by the emergency services to break through have failed. With me here is the climatologist Dr Oscar Blintz, author of the book *Climate Change and the Way We Live*."

Even as they watched, the picture began to flicker and break up into tiny squares.

"Where's Dad?" asked Greg.

"Oh he's out back with our visitor," Mum replied.

Lewis felt a tingle of dread. "Visitor? It's not Larry O'Keefe, is it?"

"No," said Mum, "His name is Spanner or something."

"Spanner?" said Greg.

"Or Screwdriver, something like that," said Mum. She tossed the remote control aside. "This is hopeless. Tell you what, Susie, why don't we have a mug of hot chocolate and watch a DVD?"

"That would be brilliant, Mrs Mac," Susie replied. "Have you got any chocolate digestives? I'm starved."

While Mum and Susie disappeared into the kitchen, Lewis and Greg grabbed their coats and hats from the hallway. They pulled them on as they went out through the back garden where Dad was standing in his overcoat and his old tweed bonnet, puffing on his pipe. The garage door was wide open. Inside, a broad-shouldered stranger was rummaging around among the tools and piles of old furniture.

"This is Mr Sven Mallet," Dad explained. "He says we have something that belongs to him. Mr Mallet, these are my two sons, Greg and Lewis."

Mallet waved an acknowledgment without looking round. He had long blond hair and was dressed in jeans and a leather vest. He was barely more than five feet tall but he was nearly that broad with muscles that bulged as he heaved the big lawnmower out of the garage. He set it aside as if it weighed nothing.

"He must have a screw loose, walking around in a blizzard dressed like that," Greg muttered aside to Lewis.

"Aren't you getting kind of chilly in that outfit, Mr Mallet?" Lewis asked their visitor.

"I don't much feel the cold," Mallet answered in a thick foreign accent. He turned just enough for them to glimpse a round, ruddy face with a short cropped beard before he returned to his search.

"What kind of an accent is that?" asked Greg. "Russian?"

"Scandinavian, I think," said Lewis.

Greg leaned close to Dad and said, "Where did he come from? He looks like he's lost his motor bike."

"He just turned up at the front door," said Dad. "Said he'd lost something around here and could he have a look in the garage."

"That's a bit odd, isn't it?" said Lewis.

Dad shrugged. "He seems harmless enough, and I didn't like to turn somebody away in this weather. Any luck yet, Mr Mallet?" he asked raising his voice.

At that point a gust of wind caused the garage door to swing down and clang shut with the visitor inside. Greg caught hold of the handle and tried to swing the door open, but it wouldn't budge.

"It's jammed again," he said.

"Are you all right in there, Mr Mallet?" Dad called out.

The answer was a heavy blow from inside that made the heavy metal door shiver.

"Boys, I think we'd better stand back," Dad advised.

The three of them beat a hasty retreat just in time. The next instant a powerful blow sent the door flying up with a clang. Sven Mallet stepped out, his round face alight. "Ja! Ja! Here it is!" he exclaimed excitedly.

In his hand he held a large metal hammer. Lewis saw it was inlaid with Norse runes. Mallet heaved the hammer into the air and declared, "At last Mjolnir is mine again!"

"I've never seen that before," said Dad, bemused.

Mallet tossed the hammer back and forth from hand to hand, beaming joyfully.

Lewis swallowed hard. "I think I know who this guy is," he said.

"Let me take a guess," said Greg. "Rumpelstiltskin?"

"He's Thor," said Lewis, "the god of thunder."

"Oh great," said Greg. "As if the weather wasn't bad enough!"

4. YOUR OWN PERSONAL AVALANCHE

"What's that, son?" Dad queried. "Thor, you say?"

"What I mean, Dad, is that he looks like a picture of Thor in one of my mythology books," Lewis explained hastily.

"I expect half the engineers in Norway look like that," said Dad. "You did say you were from Norway, didn't you, Mr Mallet?"

"Something like that," said the newcomer. "And call me Sven."

"Dad, why don't we take *Sven* inside for a cup of tea," Greg suggested.

"Good idea," Dad agreed. "You take care of that while I have a few more puffs on the old pipe."

There was no smoking allowed in the house, so Dad was always glad of an excuse to step outside with his pipe, even on a day like this.

"Come on, Sven," said Lewis, leading the blond-haired man inside. "I'll make some tea."

"Have you any foodstuffs?" Mallet asked. "A whole

roast boar I could eat."

"We can probably manage some sandwiches," said Greg.

They could hear Mum and Susie laughing over their hot chocolate in the front room. They were watching one of the *Ice Age* films. Greg directed their visitor upstairs. "Head up to the first room on the left. That's mine. We'll be up shortly."

The stranger marched up the steps, swinging his hammer at his side. Greg and Lewis took off their coats and hats and went into the kitchen.

"Are you sure he's Thor?" asked Greg as he rummaged in the fridge for cheeses and slices of cold meat. "Another Norse god? You'd think he'd be taller."

"Just because somebody's important, it doesn't mean they have to be tall," said Lewis, who was a little sensitive about his own height. "Didn't you see how short Garth Makepeace was in that photo?"

"I can't say I paid him much mind once I'd spotted Loki."

Susie bustled in to mix herself a fresh mug of chocolate. "So how's it going, boys?" she asked. "Have you dug up anything new?"

"We're working on it," said Lewis evasively.

Susie stirred her chocolate and took a sip. "You

know, I've been giving this business some thought, and it may not be as big a deal as you make out."

"Is that so?" said Greg.

"Susie, there's a packet of bourbon creams in the cupboard," Mum called through from the other room.

"Got you, Mrs Mac," Susie replied. She turned back to Greg. "Look, this O'Keefe might only be here on a scouting expedition. Maybe he'll just nose around town for a while, then fly back to Pluto."

"If he's only scouting," said Lewis, "then why all the snow?"

Susie rolled her eyes. "I already told you, he's from an ice planet. Don't you listen? He's adapted the environment to suit his alien metabolism, that's all."

She grabbed the bourbon creams out of the cupboard and headed back to the TV. "Let me know if anything turns up," she said as the kitchen door closed behind her.

"It worries me that she sounds more sensible than we do," Lewis muttered.

"That's only because she doesn't understand what's really going on," said Greg.

Lewis collected a big bottle of Irn-Bru and three plastic tumblers while Greg threw together an assortment of sandwiches. They took them upstairs on a tray and found Thor asleep on Greg's bed. The rune-carved hammer lay on the floor at his side.

As Lewis cleared space on the desk to set the tray down, Greg took the hammer by its handle and tried to lift it. It wouldn't budge. "It weighs a ton," he grunted. "What did he call it?"

"Mjolnir," said Lewis. "That was the name of Thor's hammer in the Norse myths."

Greg gave up and left the hammer on the carpet. "And what exactly was it doing in our garage?" he asked.

"I suppose we could ask him," Lewis suggested.

"Mr Mallet, time to wake up," Greg said. When there was no response he raised his voice. "Yo, Thor! Wakey wakey!"

The visitor sat straight up and blinked at the boys. "Call me Sven," he yawned. He swung his short, heavily muscled legs around so he was sitting on the edge of the bed.

"But you are Thor, right? The god of thunder?" Lewis asked.

"I sure am. But usually it's a bad idea to go around telling folk that."

Greg presented Thor with the plate of sandwiches. The god of thunder took two cheese and pickle and munched on them hungrily.

"You were quick to spot who I am," he said between bites. "Most people don't have belief in the old gods."

"You're not the first god we've met," said Lewis.

"A few months ago we had a run in with Loki," said Greg as he poured them each a tumbler of Irn-Bru.

"Loki! That wormbag!" Anger flashed in Thor's eyes. He crammed the rest of his sandwiches into his mouth, chewed furiously, then washed them down with a swallow of Irn-Bru.

Lewis took a bite of his sandwich and almost gagged. "Ugh! There are sardines in this! You know I can't stand sardines."

"I didn't force you to take that one," said Greg, biting into a ham and tomato. "You should be more careful."

"I'll have that if you're done with it," offered Thor.

Lewis passed him the sandwich and watched it disappear. He took a sip from his tumbler and said, "Loki told us he was tossed out of Asgard and exiled on Earth. He said the other gods disappeared or fell asleep or something."

"He didn't tell the whole story, then," said Thor. "For vengeance, Loki went to his cousin Surtur, the fire demon, and persuaded him to steal the Treasures of Asgard. Mjolnir was one of those treasures."

He tapped a forefinger against the handle of his hammer. "Surtur brought the treasures to Midgard – what you call Earth – and hid them in secret locations all over the world. My father Odin and I and the rest of the gods pursued Surtur and slew him… but in the battle, the Bifrost was destroyed."

"The beef roast?" said Greg. "What's that got to do with anything?"

"The Bifrost," Lewis explained. "It was the rainbow bridge that connected Asgard, the home of the gods, with Earth."

"Ja," said Thor, nodding. "With the Bifrost destroyed we were cut off from Asgard, which is the source of our power. Trapped on Earth, we became like normal folk, except that we live on for centuries."

"Are you all housemates or something?" asked Greg.

"No, we have scattered all over," said Thor. "The last I heard of any of them, Heimdall was working as a security guard and Freya had opened a bakery."

"What about the treasures?" asked Lewis.

"They too lost their power," said Thor, "and slept on in their hidden places. But a few months ago, all of a sudden I became aware that the power of the treasures had been restored and that they had been all pulled together into one place."

"St Andrews," said Greg. "But how?"

"It must have been the Lokiday spell," said Lewis. "The one Loki tricked us into casting that brought back his special day. Loki was magically transported here from Las Vegas. The same thing must have happened to the treasures."

"And the magic charged them up again," said Greg.

"That sounds about right," Thor agreed. "They are now hidden all around St Andrews. Because of my special bond with Mjolnir, I felt it call to me, even though I was far out at sea."

"What were you doing at sea?" asked Greg.

"Working on an oil rig," said Thor. "A fellow has to make a living. It took me a long time to track the hammer to St Andrews. I sure didn't expect the weather to be this bad."

"It's not supposed to be like this," said Lewis. "This is Loki's doing."

"Loki!" exclaimed Thor, his beard bristling. "Is that hogsbreath here in town?"

"He's here, all right," said Greg. "He opened the Fumblewinter Box."

"Fimbulwinter," Lewis corrected him.

Thor smacked his fist against the pillow and boomed. "Gotterdamerung!" He looked at the brothers and added, "Pardon my language, boys, but this means big trouble."

"He told us the Troll King made the box for him," said Lewis, "so I suppose he was able to track it the same way you tracked your hammer."

"So tell us, Sven, why has he started this blizzard?" Greg asked.

"He is one tricky snake," Thor scowled. "He must have some mischief in mind."

"Yes, we figured that much out for ourselves," said Greg.

"He said he wanted to keep everybody off the streets so they wouldn't get in his way," prompted Lewis.

Thor bit into a fresh sandwich, his brow knotted in thought.

Greg leaned over to Lewis and murmured, "You know, even after all we've been through, it still feels weird to have the god of thunder sitting on my bed, eating a cheese and pickle sandwich."

"The Treasures of Asgard," said Thor at last. He nodded slowly to himself. "He wants to grab all the treasures for himself. He is searching the town for them."

"Hang on, you said you could find the hammer because it belonged to *you*," Greg objected. "How is Loki going to find the treasures if they don't belong to him?"

Thor picked up Mjolnir and laid it in his lap. "The treasures all have an affinity with each other. You can use one to detect the others."

"With just one treasure he's already buried St

Andrews in snow," said Lewis. "Just think the damage he'll cause if he gets all of them."

"Then we need to go and stop him right now," said Greg, springing to his feet.

"You're right, boys," Thor agreed. "We shall be allies in the battle against the evil one." He thrust his clenched fist out towards them. Greg grinned and bumped his own fist against it and Lewis followed suit.

"For the honour of Asgard!" Thor declared.

"Right on!" Greg said. "We're coming for you now, Loki!"

"We sure are," Thor agreed. "But is it all right if I freshen up first? I've had a long journey."

"Come on," said Lewis, "I'll show you where the bathroom is."

Leaving Greg to polish off the last of the sandwiches, Lewis led Thor into the hallway and showed him where to find the bathroom. Thor walked over and put a hand on the door handle.

The instant he opened the door, a torrent of snow burst out of the bathroom and slammed him against the wall with the force of an avalanche. Thor slumped to the floor and disappeared under a mound of white.

Spilling out with the snow came the contents of the room: toothbrushes, sponges, Dad's shaver, toothpaste, shampoo, Mum's hairdryer, the toilet brush, soap, flannels, towels, a rubber duck, face cream, shower gel, and a dozen other toiletries.

The noise brought Greg rushing out to where Lewis stood frozen in shock. He gaped at the scene. "What's going on? Where's Thor?"

Lewis pointed numbly to where their visitor had disappeared.

"How could you let this happen?" Greg demanded.

"How is it my fault?" Lewis exclaimed. "All I did was show him where the toilet was."

"I leave you in charge for a few seconds," grumbled Greg, jumping on to the snow, "and he ends up buried under his own personal avalanche."

Lewis joined him and they dug with their bare hands, ignoring the chill in their fingers. Once they had cleared Thor's head they could see he was breathing but unconscious. Pausing for breath, Lewis suddenly became aware of a cold draft gusting down the back of his neck, and turned in the direction of the bathroom.

"The window must have blown open," he said.

"Even so," said Greg, clearing snow off Thor's broad shoulders, "all that snow couldn't have piled up in there by itself."

Just then the snow beneath them convulsed. It threw them to the floor with a violent heave, like a wild horse tossing a rider off its back.

Scrambling to his knees, Greg cried, "Now what?"

"It's Loki's snow magic!" gasped Lewis. "He knows where we live, remember?"

Before their horrified gaze the mound of snow was rising up, forming an animal shape like an enormous bear, with sharp icicle teeth and wicked claws.

"Thor! Sven! Wake up!" Greg yelled desperately.

The god of thunder did not stir as the monster reared over him, its frozen jaws opening wide.

5. CHRISTMAS LIGHTS

Lewis and Greg got to their feet and stared in horror. Only one of the creature's arms was fully formed and its lower half was still a shapeless mass of snow. When they took a step towards it, it turned its glassy eyes on them and lashed out with its single claw.

The boys reeled back in shock.

"I bet you wish I'd built that flamethrower now," said Greg.

"We need something to stop it before it's finished forming," said Lewis, his eyes darting around the bathroom items strewn across the floor. "There's the thing!" he exclaimed, diving for Mum's hairdryer.

He rammed the plug into the nearest socket, flipped the switch to maximum, and turned the stream of hot air on the monster. The ice beast recoiled from the heat and let out an angry crackle.

"Keep it on its face!" said Greg. "It doesn't like that."

Getting as close as he dared, Lewis directed the drier at the bear-like face. The eyes and teeth began to grow watery, but when the monster twisted away they grew solid again.

"This is just stalling it," said Lewis. "It's not strong enough to melt it."

"We need more firepower," said Greg.

The wind whipped through the open door of the bathroom, casting a flurry of snowflakes over them.

"I've got it!" Greg declared. "Lewis, you keep it distracted while I make my move."

Shaking with nerves, Lewis inched closer, thrusting the hairdryer at the monster's face. He ducked as an angry claw slashed the air above his head.

At that moment Greg launched himself past the creature into the bathroom. He slithered across the snow and struggled towards the shower where he wrenched the shower head out of its fixture. He turned the water full on and twisted the temperature control to maximum.

Stretching the shower cord as far as it would go, he fired the jet of water at the ice beast. The heating had been on all day, so the water was boiling. It blasted through the creature, forcing a screech from its melting jaws. Clouds of steam billowed through the hallway as the animal features dissolved in the hot spray.

When Thor stirred into consciousness all that was left of the monster was a single arm standing on end, poking its claw at him. The thunder god growled, and with one blow of his brawny fist smashed it to fragments.

"I think we're done," said Lewis, switching off the hairdryer.

Greg replaced the shower head and switched off the water. Then he slammed the bathroom window shut.

"Well, that sure was a surprise," said Thor, standing up and brushing the snow off himself.

Susie came bounding up the stairs and stopped when she saw the floor. "Hey, did you guys just have a water fight?" she asked. Then she spotted Thor, who was kicking some slush off his boots. "Is that the guy your mum said was poking about in the garage? Sven something or other?"

"He's Thor," said Greg. "You know, the god of thunder. But I suppose you could try to persuade him he's an alien."

"I don't need to persuade him," said Susie. "He *knows*."

Thor picked up a towel off the floor and started drying his hair. "Call me Sven."

Dad appeared at the top of the stairs. "What's happened here?" he asked mildly. "Have the pipes burst?"

"Not exactly," said Lewis. As usual, he was amazed at how calmly their dad took everything.

Dad eyed his two sons. "Maybe it's my suspicious nature," he said, "but is there something going on around here that I should know about?"

"You wouldn't believe us if we told you," said Greg.

"Don't be so sure of that. I believe a lot of strange things. I saw the Loch Ness Monster once, when I was about your age."

"Really, Dad?" said Lewis.

"Of course, it might just have been a log floating in the water," said Dad. "Either way, I wish I'd had my camera."

Lewis caught Greg's eye. He decided to take the plunge and come clean. "Dad," he began, "that time a few months back, when you were away in Wales, a lot of strange things happened here."

"How do you mean strange?" asked Dad.

Greg jumped in. "Crazy, weird, whacked out, completely off the wall," he said. "You know, totally fruit and nuts."

"Is that right?" said Dad. "Your mother didn't mention anything about it when I got back."

"Nobody remembers except us," said Lewis.

"And this guy who's calling himself Larry O'Keefe was behind it all," said Greg.

"Ja, that villain must be stopped," said Thor, shaking his fist.

"Larry O'Keefe, a villain?" said Dad. "He seemed a nice enough chap." He reached absentmindedly for his pipe before remembering he was indoors.

"Mr Mac," Susie cut in, "the boys are a bit mixed up, but there is something totally weird going on. If you ask me, it's aliens."

"Nobody asked you, Spinny," said Greg.

At that moment the lights all over the house flickered and went out.

"Whoa! Blackout!" exclaimed Susie.

"The water must have got into the wiring," Dad observed. "I expect that's done for the central heating as well."

"We'll freeze to death if we stay here then," said Greg.

"It's obviously not safe here anyway," Lewis pointed out.

"That much is for sure," said Thor.

"You can all come to our place till your electricity's fixed," Susie offered.

"That's very kind of you, Susie," said Dad. "But will your mum and dad be all right with that?"

"Oh, they love company," Susie assured him. She pulled out her phone and tried to call home. "Still no signal. But it won't matter. They're always inviting folk to stay. They say the house feels empty since Frankie and Toni moved out."

Susie's older brother Francis was a data analyst in London and her older sister Antonia was spending the summer working in Colorado. "If you're *quite* certain about that," said Mr McBride, "we wouldn't say no."

"It might be best to have another base for operations, too," said Greg. "One Larry O'Keefe doesn't know about."

"What's going on up there?" Mum called from below. "What's happened to the lights?"

"The power's out," answered Dad. "We're going over to the Spinettis."

Everybody packed a bag and they set out on foot. Dad judged it wasn't worth getting the car stuck in the snow when the Spinettis only lived two streets away.

The snow was up to their knees now and they had to help each other struggle along. Only Thor seemed to find it easy going; he insisted on carrying Mum's bag. As they turned into Rivermill Gardens, they saw a coloured pattern sparkling up ahead, like a network of tiny stars.

"Oh look!" Mum exclaimed. "They've put up Christmas lights!"

"That's just like my mum," said Susie with a grin.

The Spinetti house was decked in brilliant lights of red, green, yellow and blue and the windows were framed with tinsel. It was a big house and the Spinettis had added some extensions, including a storeroom filled with sporting goods for their business.

Susie pushed open the door and whipped off her fur hat as she stepped inside. "Mum! Dad! It's me! I've got the McBrides with me!"

Two boys of five and six came hopping down the stairs and rushed at them waving plastic swords. "Invaders!" they cried.

"Clear off, you two!" laughed Susie, blocking their swords with her hockey stick.

After a brief tussle the boys retreated back up the stairs and stood there brandishing their swords menacingly. From the other end of the hall Mrs Spinetti came bustling out of the kitchen in a brightly coloured apron decorated with reindeer. She was a round, rosy-faced woman whose black curls tumbled over her shoulders.

"Adele!" she exclaimed, smiling at Mrs McBride. "I wasn't expecting to see you. I wasn't expecting to see anybody in this weather."

"Our electricity broke down," Mum explained.

"I said they could come here till it was fixed," said Susie.

"Of course they can," said Mrs Spinetti. "And who's this fine figure of a man?"

"Which one of us do you mean?" Dad joked.

"The chap with the muscles, of course," said Mrs Spinetti.

"This is Sven," said Dad. "He's an engineer."

"Come to fix your boiler, has he?" said Mrs Spinetti.

"That's right," said Thor, "but the parts can't be got with this weather."

"He's a Viking raider!" one of the boys shouted over the bannister, pointing his sword at Thor.

"Michael, you and Charlie put those swords away and go fetch a board game," their mother ordered them. "Susie, can you dig out some Christmas music?"

"On it, Mum," said Susie, stripping off her coat and chasing her brothers upstairs. "Are there any stovies left?" she shouted down.

"I'll see what I can scrape off the bottom of the pot," her mother called back. "Come and have a cherry brandy, Adele. There's hot blackcurrant cordial for the boys."

"It looks like you've decorated the whole house," said Mum, looking at the tinsel and lights that were draped over the mirror and the family photographs.

"Well, if you can't stop the snow, you might as well enjoy it," said Mrs Spinetti. "Besides, I'll let you in on a secret. We keep a wee Christmas tree in our bedroom all year round. I like to see the lights twinkle."

She took Mr McBride by the arm and directed him

to the back of the house. "Come along, Alan," she said. "George is in the laundry room tending to his home brewed beer. It will make his day if you sample a glass."

"Oh, I think I could put myself out that far for a friend," said Dad.

Lewis, Greg and Thor were soon settled around a table in the music room where Mr Spinetti kept his guitars and banjo. They had cups of hot blackcurrant and a plate heaped with slices of Mrs Spinetti's home-baked gingerbread.

Mum ducked her head in and said, "If you lot are happy here, Theresa and I are popping out for a bit."

"Popping out?" said Lewis. "In this blizzard?"

"What are you going to do?" asked Greg. "Hunt caribou?"

Mrs Spinetti appeared behind Mum. "There's a lot of old folks in this neighbourhood," she said. "We're going to take them some cake and make sure they're all right."

When they were gone Greg and Lewis looked at each other. "Well, if Mum and Mrs Spinetti are out helping people," said Greg, "I suppose we need to do our bit to save the world."

Lewis nodded and turned to Thor. "All right, Sven, you say Loki is here to collect the Treasures of Asgard. You'd better let us know what we're up against."

"We know about your hammer and Loki's box," said Greg. "What else is there?"

"Well, let's see," said Thor, pondering. "There's the Falcon Cloak, the Iron Gauntlets, the Spear Gungnir, the Sword Hofud, the Shoes of Vidar, the Bone of Ullr, the Gjallahorn, the Yggdrasil Seed, the Golden Apples, the Ring Draupnir, the Shield Svalin..."

"Okay, okay," Greg cut in, "we get the picture. There's a lot of stuff out there."

"And if Loki gets his hands on it all, he might be unstoppable," said Lewis.

"So we've got to get to them first," said Greg.

"That's right," Thor agreed. "I can track them with Mjolnir, but it will take time."

"Plus we have to find a way to get through the snow," Lewis pointed out. "It must be waist-high by now."

"I can help with that," said Susie. She was standing in the doorway munching on a packet of cheese and onion crisps.

"Spinny, we appreciate the hospitality," said Greg, "but unless you've got a snowmobile, you'd better leave the hard work to us."

Susie polished off the last crisp and crushed the empty packet in her hand. "Excuse me, but who was it that saved the two of you from that ice monster this morning?" she demanded. "If not for me, he'd have whisked you off through space and buried you in a mine on Japetus."

"Ja-what?" said Greg.

"Japetus," said Lewis. "It's one of the moons of Saturn."

"Thanks, Lewis," said Greg, his voice dripping with sarcasm. "That's a really useful piece of information."

"Besides," said Susie, bouncing the crumpled packet off Greg's nose, "with all your airy fairy ideas, you need somebody with a good head on her shoulders."

Thor nodded approvingly. "Susie has the spirit of a true warrior."

"You see?" beamed Susie. "Sven's on my side."

"All right, Spinny, you win," Greg conceded. "You're on the team. But don't forget who's in charge."

"It's not you, is it?" Susie smirked. "We're in enough trouble as it is."

"We still haven't sorted out how we're going to get across town," Lewis reminded them.

"That's what I was going to tell you," said Susie. "We've got skis, enough for all of us. We can ski right down the Canongate."

"That's fine, Spinny," said Greg, "but it's all uphill after that. What are we supposed to do? Attach rockets to our backs?"

"Oh I can come up with something better than that, for sure," said Thor. "Remember I have Mjolnir."

"How is a hammer going to help?" asked Lewis.

"I'll show you. Susie, where are the skis?"

Susie led Thor off to the storeroom at back of the house where Mr Spinetti kept his supply of sporting goods. They returned with four pairs of skis. Susie was wearing a backpack. She hooked her thumbs through the straps and watched as Thor singled out one of the skis and examined it closely.

"Wood laminate with a strip of aluminium," he murmured. "That will do fine."

He touched his hammer to the tip of the ski and slowly drew it down the whole length. He did the same with all four sets of skis.

"Right, now we are ready to go," he declared.

"What did you just—" Lewis began, but Thor raised a hand to silence him.

"Better just do as he says," Susie advised. "He knows his stuff."

As they headed for the door, Dad appeared with a glass of home brew in his hand. "Skis, eh? Would somebody like to clue me in?" he asked.

"I must catch that scoundrel Loki," said Thor, patting the hammer that was stuck in his belt.

"He means Larry O'Keefe, Dad," said Greg. "Sven's kind of a policeman, you know, from Swedenborg."

"I suppose Larry's been involved in some kind of

financial scandal?" said Dad. "Made off with some share certificates, has he?"

"Something like that," said Lewis.

"Sven needs our help to find his way around town," said Greg.

"That's right," Thor confirmed.

"Don't worry about us, Dad," said Lewis. "We'll be fine."

Dad took a slow sip of his beer. "I only worry about you when you're apart," he told them. "Each of you has his own kind of trouble he can get into. Together, though, I reckon you can cope with pretty much anything."

"Really?" said Lewis. "I never knew you thought that."

"What about you, Supergirl?" Mr McBride said to Susie. "Will I tell your dad you've gone skiing?"

"Tell him I'll be home for tea, Mr Mac," said Susie with a smile. "I always am."

Once outside in the street they strapped on the skis.

"Look, I know we won't sink in the snow with these on," said Lewis, "but it's going to take us a long time waddling across town like this."

"And shouldn't we have poles," asked Greg, "you know, to push ourselves along with?"

"Sven says we won't need them," answered Susie.

"Form a line behind me," Thor instructed them.

Once they had lined up behind him, Thor lofted his hammer into the air. Immediately Lewis felt a tremor run down the length of his skis.

"Hey, what's going on?" said Greg. "It feels like there's a current running through these things."

In front of them, Thor coasted effortlessly forward. It was as if his skis were moving across the snow under their own power. With a jerk Lewis, Greg and Susie found themselves sliding along the street after him.

"The skis are alive!" Lewis exclaimed.

"Better hold on to your hats, boys!" Susie grinned.

6. A WOLF, A SNAKE, AND AN ICE MAID

Snow swirled about them as they gathered speed.

"You see, Spinny, it's magic," Greg called over his shoulder to Susie.

"Don't be daft," Susie called back. "It's magnetism. He magnetised the aluminium in the skis and now he's controlling them with his hammer."

Lewis clutched his hat. "Sven, do we have to go so fast?" he pleaded.

They were shooting down the Canongate Road so quickly he could hardly catch his breath. When they reached the bottom, instead of slowing down, the skis gathered speed and rocketed up the other side. At the top they shot five feet in the air and flumped down on the snow, still racing along.

Lewis groaned. "This is worse than the Whizeroo ride you made me go on at the Lammas Fair."

"Don't you dare throw up this time, Lewis," Greg told him.

They swerved right, shooting under the arch of the

West Port into South Street. Lights glimmered in some of the shop windows, but the snow-covered street was deserted. Everyone was shut away safely indoors.

Thor was holding Mjolnir straight out in front of him. "The tug is very strong, like there are two treasures in the one place."

"It must be Loki," said Greg. "He's got the box and he's closing in on the next treasure."

They sped past the empty shell of the old Greyfriars chapel on their right. Before them on their left the spire of Holy Trinity church was capped with snow like a mountain peak.

"He's dead ahead of us now," Thor reported.

"It looks like we're headed straight for the cathedral," said Susie.

Between the east end of the town and the harbour lay St Andrews' medieval cathedral. It had been abandoned centuries ago and left to fall into ruins. Since then the enclosed grounds had served as a graveyard, but its surviving twin towers still made it an impressive monument. The encircling wall was heaped up with piles of snow, like ramparts raised to repel invaders. The gate was completely blocked up.

"We are going over," Thor announced.

They skied right up the snowy rampart and came to an abrupt halt at the top. Lewis' stomach lurched sickeningly and it took a moment for him to take in the sight below. The cathedral grounds had been cleared, with piles of snow heaped up here and there between tombstones dappled with frost and lichen. No snowflakes were falling here, but a cold mist had blown in from the harbour to wind itself around the ruins.

"Loki had to move the snow so he can look for the treasure," Thor observed. "Come on, we're going down."

They slid down the other side, removed their skis and piled them up near the gate where a tall, skinny tower marked their position.

"Have you any idea which of the treasures he's after?" asked Lewis.

Thor shrugged and gestured at the mist with Mjolnir. "All I know is that one of the treasures is hidden out there and Loki seeks it."

"Then let's go and spoil his fun," said Greg.

They walked through an arch into an area, now open to the sky, that had once been the interior of the cathedral. To their right reared the old south wall, still mostly intact, while to their left ran a line of flat, circular stones, the bases of the pillars that had once supported the long-vanished roof. Beyond these were rows of gravestones matted with moss and flecked with frost.

Lewis peered ahead where he could just make out the towers of the east gable poking up through the mist like a pair of horns.

"It's a bit creepy, isn't it, what with the mist and all," said Susie. "Just the spot for a ghost story."

"I think we've enough on our plate without ghosts, Spinny," said Greg.

"Shhh!" said Lewis. "I think I hear something."

They stopped in their tracks and listened. Through the chilly, misty air came a ponderous *crunch*. A heartbeat later, there came another crunch. A third followed, heavier and closer.

"Something bad's coming," said Susie, clutching her hockey stick tightly.

Thor turned towards the sound. "*Gotterdamerung!*" he exclaimed.

Marching towards them through an opening in the wall was a twelve-foot tall warrior woman made entirely of ice. Her face was a sharply contoured skull and her hair a mass of icicles hanging down the back of her head. An armour of glassy scales covered her body and in her frozen hands she gripped a spear of ice.

A savage hiss issued from her blue lips and with a sudden spring she launched herself into their midst. Lewis ducked with a yelp and rolled away as she stabbed at him.

"Try picking on somebody that's armed!" Susie challenged, making a lunge with her hockey stick.

The ice maiden whipped around and, with a furious sweep of her spear, dashed the stick from Susie's grasp and sent it cartwheeling through the air. Snatching Susie by the back of her jacket, Greg yanked her to safety as the ice maid planted her spear into the ground where she had been standing half a moment before.

"For goodness' sake, Spinny, will you watch yourself!" he told her.

"Get back, all of you!" Thor commanded.

They fell back behind the burly Norseman as he confronted the ice maiden with his hammer.

A stream of icy vapour issued from the monster's nostrils. Lifting her spear high, she reared back and drove it at Thor's heart. Incredibly, Thor sidestepped the thrust. With a lightning swirl of his hammer he dashed the spear to pieces.

The ice maid's jagged features contorted in fury. Her skeletal hands sprouted claws like daggers and she took a savage swipe at her enemy.

Thor dodged again and crashed his hammer into her leg. The icy limb burst apart under the impact and the creature toppled over.

With inhuman determination, she crawled forward and caught Thor's ankle in her talons. Instead of trying to shake free, Thor raised Mjolnir and brought it down on her head. The icy skull shattered into a thousand pieces and the monster's body went still. Thor kicked the motionless fingers, snapping them apart.

"Nice going, Sven!" exclaimed Susie.

"You don't mess with the god of thunder," said Greg, giving Thor a congratulatory pat on the back. "If that's the best Loki's got, this will be a piece of cake."

Susie retrieved her hockey stick and stuck it through the straps of her backpack.

"Stay alert," Thor warned. "If I know Loki – and I have known him for about two thousand years – he has more surprises in store for us."

They moved warily onward through the ruins until the wall to their right ended and beyond it they could make out the square bulk of St Rule's Tower. As they paused to look about them a fresh cloud of mist blew in and enveloped them.

"I can't see a thing!" fumed Greg. He waved a hand as if trying to bat the fog away.

"Hold still," said Thor. "Don't move."

There was a tense pause. Straining his eyes in the gloom, Lewis was aware of his heart beating rapidly. All at once Greg clapped a hand on his shoulder. "There's something moving out there," he muttered.

"And moving fast," breathed Susie.

The air seemed to grow even colder and Lewis couldn't help shivering. Thor strode to the fore. The next moment, a long glistening shape, like an oil pipeline come to life, came shooting across the ground towards them with staggering speed. Before Thor could make a move, the thing whipped itself around him like a tightly-coiled spring, pinning his arms and hammer to his sides.

"It's some kind of snake!" Greg exclaimed in horror.

"Except it's *miles* long!" cried Susie.

This ice creature's body was as thick as a tree trunk and lay twined around trees and gravestones on all sides of them. A scaly head as big as a car reared up above them, baring a pair of fangs like bayonets.

"I can't move!" Thor grunted, straining in vain against the monster's coils. "Run, before it gets you!"

They fell back as the monster took a snap at them. "Don't worry, Sven," said Susie, reaching into her pack. "I've got this covered."

"Got it covered?" Greg gasped. "Spinny, what are you talking about?"

"This!" Susie declared, holding up a small red rod.

"What's that, a flare?" asked Lewis.

Susie bobbed her head. "Campers carry them so they can signal for help if they run into trouble. We had one left in the store room."

"Enough talk, Spinny," said Greg. "Light it!"

Before Susie could act, the giant snake's tail came sweeping across the ground and whipped her legs out from under her. With a yelp of surprise, she went flying backwards and the flare tumbled out of her hand.

"Susie!" Greg yelled, dashing to her side. He seized her by the hand and pulled her to her feet.

Lewis saw the flare rolling across the grass and made a dive for it, but the snake was faster. A flick of its tail whacked the rod into the air. The flare flew off and disappeared into the mist.

The great serpent lunged at Greg and Susie, eyes glittering like diamonds. They flung themselves aside in opposite directions as the ferocious fangs stabbed the air between them.

"Get away!" Thor yelled at them. His face was crimson with the effort of trying to struggle free, but the snake had him locked tight.

Lewis peered into the mist, hoping to spot where the flare had landed. As he did so, the serpent tail smacked him in the back and sent him tumbling head over heels. He rolled to a bruising halt at the base of a headstone, panting in the freezing air. As he groped around dazedly for his bearings, his hand encountered a tubular object.

The flare!

He snatched it up in shaking fingers and struggled to his feet. He opened his mouth to shout for the others, but was struck dumb as he saw a new threat materialise out of the drifting bank of fog.

Padding towards him, big as a horse and made entirely of ice, was a wolf. Its ears were folded back and it bared its icicle teeth in a vicious snarl. The crystal facets of its eyes flashed hungrily.

Lewis backed off, brandishing the flare in front of him in the faint hope that the sight of it would keep the creature at bay. He racked his brains to think of how to light it, but his mind was a blank. Still retreating, he bumped against cold, rough stonework, and realised he was trapped against a wall. The wolf kept padding slowly towards him, as though relishing his fear.

Lewis clutched the flare in trembling fingers, his mind frozen in terror.

"Hang on, Lewis!" cried a voice.

It was Susie, pelting towards him with her hockey stick in her hands. The wolf swung about to face her with a gravelly rumble. Pulling up at the last instant, she whacked it squarely in the mouth. Shards of ice went flying, but in the next instant the wolf caught the stick in its massive jaws and snapped it in half.

"You stupid beastie!" Susie yelled angrily. She flung

aside the stump of handle that was all she had left. "Right, now I'm raging! Lewis, toss me that flare!"

Shaking off his panic, Lewis threw the flare and Susie caught it in one hand. She pulled the cap off the end and flipped it round in her fingers as the wolf crunched the remains of her stick into splinters. Spitting out the pieces, it opened its mouth wide and let out a horrible growl.

"You know, in Norse mythology," said Lewis, staring at the fearsome beast, "there was a wolf that ate the sun."

"Is that right?" said Susie, striking the cap against the fuse. "Let's see him eat this!"

As the flare sprouted its jet of flame she flung it with all her strength, right down the gullet of the great beast. The creature swallowed it and light blazed down into its belly. Lit up from inside, the wolf convulsed, snapping its jaws and staggering from side to side. Its body exploded and fell to the ground in pieces that dissolved into puddles as the flare fizzled out.

Breathing hard, Lewis turned to Susie. "Sorry about your hockey stick."

"It was a classic stick," sighed Susie, "even with all the nicks."

"Do you have any more flares?" Lewis asked. "We still have to rescue Thor from that snake."

Susie shook her head glumly. "That was the only one. And that big worm's still haring about the place like a runaway train."

"So how do we stop it?"

The question was no sooner out of his mouth than they heard a cry of "Gangway! Leg it!"

They looked round and saw Greg dashing towards them, his legs pumping furiously. The ice serpent was right behind him, jaws gaping, and some distance back, they could see Thor, still trapped in the freezing coils.

Lewis and Susie joined Greg in his desperate race, jumping over graves and swerving round tombstones.

"Where are we going?" gasped Lewis.

"Back to the gate," Greg puffed, "to get the skis."

"The skis?" panted Susie. "We can't run out on Sven!"

"We're not!" Greg told her. "Just do what I say!"

They skidded to a halt at the skis and Greg snatched one up. "Grab one each and get ready to throw it," he ordered.

As he picked up a ski, Lewis complained, "We can't throw hard enough to hurt that thing."

"We don't have to," said Greg. "Thor will do the rest."

The snake slithered to a halt and reared over them, bobbing its huge head this way and that as if choosing which of them to devour first. Locked in its coils, Thor kicked his legs to no avail. "Why have you stopped?" he wheezed.

"I've got a plan, Sven," Greg called back. "Get ready to use your hammer when we throw the skis your way."

Susie's eyes lit up. "I see where you're going with this."

"I wish I did," groaned Lewis, but he copied the others. They each gripped a ski in both hands and pulled it back at shoulder height. "One, two, three, *fire!*" cried Greg.

They hurled their three skis into the face of the serpent. Instead of losing momentum and dropping to the ground, the three missiles gained speed as they flew. They shot down the throat of the serpent, fast as rockets, tearing it apart from the inside like knives.

"It's Mjolnir!" Lewis exclaimed. "Thor's using its magnetic power on the skis."

"To turn them into guided missiles," said Greg, a proud grin spreading across his face.

When the skis reached the coils that held Thor prisoner, they burst the monster apart. Thor leapt free with a cry of triumph, lofting the hammer over his head. Broken fragments of the ice serpent lay all around him. A section of tail twitched three times, then it was over.

"Ka-BOOM!" cried Susie, pumping the air with her fist.

"You see, Spinny," said Greg. "All it took was a bit of Norse magic, or something."

"Pretty clever," Susie admitted, thumping him proudly on the shoulder.

They were all flushed with the excitement of the chase and dizzy with relief at their escape. Lewis leaned against a snow-covered wall until the heaving in his stomach had settled.

"We still have to find Loki," Thor reminded them.

"The mist's clearing," Lewis noticed. "That should make it easier."

"And now he doesn't have his ice monsters to protect him," said Thor with a vengeful gleam in his eye.

Once they had stacked the skis again, they advanced in a group across the cathedral grounds. The air continued to clear until they spotted Loki perched on the edge of a stone tomb near St Rule's Tower. He smirked at Thor.

"Thor, you palooka, I should have known you'd show up."

"Loki, you ratsnout, justice has come for you," Thor threatened.

"Always the blowhard," said Loki, sliding to the ground. "And look at the mess you've made of my toys. All that time I spent making them, and you've smashed them to pieces." He gestured at the scattered fragments of the ice monsters. "It was the same when we were kids, like the time you knocked down my sandcastle."

"It was full of scorpions," Thor reminded him.

"So tell me," said Loki, "what do you hear from the other gods – the old gang? Odin still a wise guy? Tyr's temper as bad as ever?"

"I don't run into them much," said Thor.

"I expect they're wandering around doing whatever it is mortals do to pass the time," said Loki. "Too bad. I'd like to see the looks on their faces when they get a load of my latest caper."

"Larry, whatever you think you're up to, it's over now," said Greg. "Why don't you hand over the treasures peacefully, before Thor has to get rough with you."

"You can probably catch the next shuttle back to the ice planet of Hoth," said Susie.

"The treasures, yes, that's what it's all about, I suppose," said Loki with a sly smile. He reached into his pocket and pulled out a gold ring, which he tossed into the air and caught. "Recognise this, meathead?"

"Ja, it's the Ring Draupnir," said Thor.

"I found it under the gravestone of a man named Bell," said Loki, holding the ring up to his eye and peering through it. "Pretty good gag, eh, *ring, bell*."

"These treasures don't belong to you, Loki," said Thor, extending a hand for the ring.

"Really?" said Loki. "What will you give me for it?"

He flipped the ring, spinning it into the air like a coin. Immediately Thor stretched out Mjolnir and frowned in concentration. The ring froze in mid-air then shot towards Thor and stuck to the head of his hammer. Thor pulled it loose and clasped it in his fist.

Loki seemed unconcerned. "I should have expected you to pull a dirty trick like that," he laughed. "You're such a killjoy."

"I don't understand," Lewis said to Greg. "Thor took the ring off him and all he does is laugh."

"Maybe he's finally snapped," said Greg. "He always was pretty batty."

Thor took a menacing step towards Loki. "And now for the reckoning," he threatened.

"Not so fast, you lummox," said Loki raising his hand. "I still have a few tricks up my sleeve."

He slid the Fimbulwinter box out of his pocket and chortled.

"Better take that off him before he conjures up any more monsters," said Lewis.

"Monsters?" said Loki. "That's kids' stuff. Try this!" He jerked a thumb over his shoulder to indicate what was coming up behind him.

"By the beard of Odin!" Thor gasped.

The three youngsters were speechless at what they saw.

A wall of snow ten metres high was rolling towards them from the far end of the cathedral. It covered the whole breadth of the grounds and was coming at them with the force of a tidal wave. Loki turned and walked towards it, the snow parting to let him pass through. They heard him laugh as he disappeared into the whiteness.

"Run!" yelled Greg.

The four of them spun round and ran as the deluge of snow swept across the cathedral to bury them.

7. THE SIGN OF THE TRICKSTER

The torrent of snow engulfed walls and tombstones, casting spumes of ice into the air at every impact. Ahead of them was the steep bank of snow piled up against the outer wall.

"Go! Go!" yelled Thor, waving them on. "I'll get the skis!"

Greg, Lewis and Susie jumped at the snowy bank, digging their feet in and clawing their way up. As they climbed, Thor grabbed the skis and hurled them two at a time high over their heads.

When he reached the top of the bank, Lewis turned, panting, to see the tidal wave of white flooding the cathedral. It overtook Thor as he was scrambling up after them and when it hit he was completely engulfed.

A flurry of flakes gusted over them as the snow crashed against the wall like a wave smashing into a rock.

"Sven!" cried Susie. "Are you okay?"

"Don't tell me he's buried again!" Greg exclaimed.

"It's still not my fault!" Lewis protested.

Feverishly scanning the sea of snow, he saw a hand sticking out. He floundered over and seized hold of it. To his relief, Thor's thick fingers twitched in his grasp. "He's alive! Now help me dig him out!" he called to the others.

Working together, they shifted the snow away. Bit by bit, the Norse god emerged. First his arm and then his thick blond hair came into view. Then his head popped clear.

He blinked the icy crystals out of his blue eyes and worked his broad shoulders loose. Reaching up with his other hand, he managed to drag himself up beside the three youngsters.

"Thanks," Thor panted. "You are worthy companions to the god of thunder."

All together they slid down the other side to land sitting on the street below. The realisation that they were safe instead of buried started them all laughing at once. Thor helped them to their feet and they stood, brushing the snow off themselves.

Lewis shivered. "Now that we're not running around, I'm *frozen*."

"You're right, Lewis," said Greg. "We need to go and warm up some place."

"Look, there's a light on in the Beacon Tea Room," said Susie, pointing down North Street. "I bet Desmond's open for business."

"Let's hope so," said Lewis. "I could do with a hot drink."

They tramped over to where the light shone brightly through the lace curtains and stacked their skis against the wall. A bell above the door tinkled as they stepped inside. There were half a dozen tables in the tea room covered with red and white checked cloths. On the walls were photographs of harbours and fishing boats.

The owner, Desmond Soutar, emerged from the back room through a beaded curtain, wearing a parka over his bright yellow shirt and scarlet tie. He pulled on a Russian style fur hat as he manoeuvred around the tables.

"Well, come on in and shut that door," he urged. "What on earth's brought you lot out in this winter wonderland?"

"It's a long story," said Greg.

"You'd have to be mad to believe it," said Susie.

"Oh, I'm halfway there already," said Desmond. "It would only take a nudge to put me over the brink."

There was the sound of a muffled voice calling down from an upper room.

"What's that, mother?" Desmond shouted back. "Yes, it's customers! Three young folk and a body builder!"

"This is Sven," said Lewis. "He's visiting from Norway."

"Brought the weather with him, hasn't he," Desmond commented. "I've been curled up under a quilt with a hot water bottle and a good book. Honestly, my blood's too thin for this weather. I should have emigrated to Australia like my brother Colin, but I suppose somebody had to stay here and take care of mother."

The muffled voice called out again.

"It's the McBride boys and the Spinetti girl!" Desmond answered.

There was another unintelligible inquiry.

"No, the younger one! The older one's away in America! And the other chap's a Norwegian!" He cast a wary eye over Mjolnir. "What's he carrying that hammer around for? Weight training?"

"He's, um, a bit of a DIY nut," said Greg. "You never know when he'll want to bash in a few nails."

"I've a cupboard door round the back that's coming off its hinges," Desmond told Thor. "Maybe you could take a look at it before you go." He blew on his hands. "Come on, sit down at this table by the heater. Even with it full on, it's a bit parky. Still, a fresh pot of tea will warm you up no end."

"We're glad to find a place that's open, Desmond," said Susie.

"Oh I expect that ghastly coffee chain will have their slaves shackled to the espresso machines on the off chance somebody staggers in from the cold," said Desmond with a grimace. "But you don't want to drink that stuff. It goes right through you, so it does. A pot of best Darjeeling is what you want."

When Desmond went off to brew the tea Greg muttered, "Could we not get a coke or something?"

"Desmond only serves tea," said Susie. "He's got about fifty different kinds."

"I don't care what we drink, as long as it's hot," said Lewis, rubbing his hands together to warm them.

Thor took out the golden ring and turned it over in his fingers.

"What did you say the ring was called again?" asked Lewis.

"Don't you know?" said Greg. "You knew all about the Beef Roast."

"*Bifrost*," said Lewis.

"It is called Draupnir," said Thor.

"And what does it do?" asked Susie. "Turn you invisible?"

"Maybe it shoots lightning," Greg suggested. "That would come in handy."

"It is a ring of knowledge," said Thor.

"Can it tell us where Loki's going to turn up next?" asked Lewis.

Thor frowned. "It's not that kind of knowledge."

"How do you mean?" said Lewis.

"Try it for yourself," said Thor, handing him the ring.

Lewis examined it. It was made of gold and there were Nordic runes inscribed on the inside. He slipped it on. "I don't get it. Nothing's happening."

"Well, what can you tell us now about the ring?" Thor prompted him.

"Not much," said Lewis. "It was forged by the dwarven brothers Brokkr and Eitri as part of a set of three gifts that also included Mjolnir and Gullibursti, the Golden Boar." He was surprised to find the words tripping from his lips of their own accord. "It was because of a bet that they couldn't fashion better gifts than the Sons of Ivaldi who..."

"Fine!" Greg interrupted. "A ring that tells you all about itself. That's really going to save the day!"

"Oh there is more to it than that," said Thor. "Tell us about this place, Lewis."

"This place? It's been the Beacon Tea Room for thirty-seven years, since Mr and Mrs Soutar moved in, though at first it was called Soutar's Café, but after her husband died Desmond's mum changed the name." All these facts were buzzing in Lewis' brain like a swarm of bees. He could hardly talk fast enough to keep up with them. "Before that it was a corner shop selling groceries and newspapers run by two sisters named Agnes and Blodwyn Fludd. When they bought it, it was a private house belonging to a leather merchant named McPherson who was moving to Glasgow to open a boot factory. His father—"

"Enough, Lewis," Greg cut in. "If you talk any faster your tongue will catch fire."

Thor reached over and plucked the ring from Lewis' finger. "You see, it lets you know everything about where you are right now."

"It taps into a local datastream," said Susie.

"Spinny, that doesn't actually mean anything," said Greg.

"Here, Lewis, you hang on to it," said Thor handing the ring back. "It will help you if we get separated."

Lewis slipped the ring into his pocket and rubbed his brow. "It's given me a really sore head," he said.

"I've got the cure for that," said Desmond setting a tray down in front of them. "There's nothing clears the head like a cup of good strong tea."

He set out the teapot, milk, sugar and four sets of cups and saucers.

"Not very busy today, are you?" said Susie, glancing at the empty tables.

"There's a few folk have struggled in, but not many. And here's Mother been baking shortbread all morning. There's barrowloads of it, so I can't let you go until you've scoffed down three squares each."

He fetched a plate piled high with shortbread from the counter and set it down in front of his customers.

There was another muffled cry from upstairs.

"Yes, Mother," Desmond called back, "I've given them some shortbread!" He poured tea into each of the cups. "She gives me no peace, you know. I have to tell her everything that's going on. I should get a job commentating on the radio, parades, royal weddings, the state opening of Parliament. I'd be good at that. Not so much at sports though. I can never spot where the ball is."

"How much do we owe you?" asked Susie, reaching into her pocket.

Desmond waved the offer aside. "There's no charge. On a day like today we're like a first-aid post – like in one of those old war films."

He disappeared through the bead curtains and they heard classical music coming from his CD player. Thor and Susie helped themselves to the lion's share of the shortbread while Greg made a grab at what was left. Lewis wrapped his hands around his cup and gratefully gulped down the hot tea.

When Desmond returned he was immediately drawn to the window where he stood staring at the sky. "Hark at this, will you! I've never seen the like of it."

Everyone got up and joined him in looking upward. Far across town the snow was forming a strange, curling pattern in the air.

"It looks like skywriting," said Desmond. "But it can't be, can it? There's no planes flying about in this."

"It looks like two snakes trying to bite each other's tails," said Lewis.

Thor rubbed his beard and his brow furrowed.

There was another call from upstairs.

"I need to go up and fetch her medicine," said Desmond. "You'll be all right, will you?"

"Yes, thanks," said Susie. "The tea was great."

"Of course it was," said Desmond. "Miles better than that Colombian sludge they serve in the coffee place down the road. That stuff gives you the runs."

He disappeared upstairs while Susie and the boys continued to stare at the snow shapes in the sky.

"It's definitely some kind of pattern," said Susie, "like those crop circles you hear about."

"What do you make of it, Sven?" asked Greg.

"The sign of the twin serpents," said Thor. "It is the symbol of Loki."

"Loki?" said Greg. "So it's kind of like Batman's bat signal then."

"It looks like it's hovering somewhere around Langlands Road," Lewis observed.

"Are you saying Loki is there under that sign, Sven?" asked Greg.

"I think so," Thor replied.

"Why would he tell us where he is?" Susie wondered. "I thought he didn't want us sticking our noses into his business."

"Maybe he wants his ring back," Greg suggested.

"It is funny, though," said Lewis, "he didn't seem that bothered about losing it."

"Not bothered?" said Greg. "Lewis, he tried to bury us alive under a mountain of snow. I'd say he was a bit bothered."

"It must be a challenge," said Thor grimly. "A challenge to combat."

"Or a trap," said Greg. "That would be more his style."

"Either way," said Thor, "we must confront him."

As they headed out the door Desmond reappeared. "I thought you were going to fix my cupboard," he called after Thor.

"We've got something else we need to fix first," said Greg, closing the door behind them.

8. MAYBE I'M AMAZED

Guided by the mystical power of Mjolnir, the magnetised skis carried them down Abbey Walk into the new town. Occasionally somebody who had ventured out for supplies caught a glimpse of them shooting by, but before they could cry out in surprise, the four skiers had disappeared round a corner. Finally they came to a halt by a snow-covered wall where the double snake symbol was hovering in the air high above.

"This is the place," said Thor pointing with his hammer.

"Here?" said Lewis. "St Andrews United football ground?"

St Andrews United were a junior team with a small but dedicated following. Their games were a big feature of the sports pages of the local paper.

"Maybe Loki wants to settle it all with a penalty shootout," Greg joked.

"I haven't been here since they beat Bo'ness in the Fife Cup," said Susie.

"When Stevens scored the winner in the last minute," Greg recalled. "What a shot!"

"Please, don't start talking about football," Lewis muttered under his breath.

Susie squinted up at the symbol in the sky overhead. "You know, this would make a pretty good landing site for his spaceship."

Thor looked perplexed. "I detect only one treasure here."

"Only one?" said Lewis. "But if Loki's here with the box, and he's come to collect another treasure, there should be two of them."

They kicked off their skis next to the entrance. The gate itself was unlocked. Pushing it open, they came to an abrupt halt.

Greg said sourly, "This is new."

The flat open turf of the football pitch had disappeared. In its place was a network of paths surrounded by high walls of murky green. The frozen path that stretched before them glistened like a sheet of glass.

"A maze!" Susie exclaimed.

Lewis turned to Thor. "Why would Loki go to the bother of making such a thing?"

"Yeah," said Greg. "If the signal's a challenge like you said, why call us out, then put an obstacle course in our way?

The god of thunder shrugged his broad shoulders. "It is another of his infernal games."

Susie shook herself like a football player coming off the bench to take the field. "Then let's get in there and win it!"

Lewis was still musing. "Why *here?*" he persisted. "What's so special about the St Andrews United ground?"

Susie paid no attention. "We'd better get a move on if we're going to grab the treasure off him! Just give me a minute to get myself sorted."

Shrugging off her backpack, she sat down on the ground and hauled out a set of brightly polished ice-skating blades. She briskly slotted them into a set of grooves on the soles of her boots and secured them with metal clamps.

"I had a notion these would come in handy," she said.

She glided out onto the ice-covered path and did a double pirouette.

"That's enough showing off, Spinny," said Greg. "Don't you skate off on your own and get lost."

"Mjolnir will be our guide," Thor announced, "so I will go in front."

Susie slid aside to let him pass, then waved the brothers forward. Gripping each other by the shoulder, they shuffled forward, not daring to lift their feet from the ice.

The path proved as slippery as it looked. Three steps from the entrance, Lewis' feet almost shot out from under him and only Greg's tight grasp kept him from a tumble. Twenty paces further on the path brought them to a T-junction. Clasping the haft of Mjolnir before him in both hands, Thor paused and shut his eyes.

A moment later he opened them and pointed left. "That is the way we must go."

Each time they came to a branching path, Thor paused to choose the route. They were approaching a four-way crossing when there came a sudden rush of footsteps. A familiar figure in a fur coat and fedora hat flashed past in front of them, right through the crossroads.

"Loki!" Greg and Lewis exclaimed together as the man in the hat vanished round a corner.

Thor spat out an angry Nordic curse and launched himself after his enemy. In his warlike haste he lost his footing and went down with a heavy thud. As the god skidded helplessly across the ice on his belly, Greg and Lewis hurried forward to help him but slipped and fell right on top of him.

"One side, you lot!" cried Susie. "Skater coming through!"

She skated past them in a whoosh of cold air and swerved round the corner after Loki.

"She can't take on Loki by herself," said Greg as he and Lewis struggled up and hoisted Thor to his feet.

They took the same route Loki and Susie had, but almost at once they were faced with more choices. Every few metres a fresh path branched off.

"This place is impossible," said Greg.

"But if there isn't another treasure here," said Lewis, "what is going on? Why is he leading us on this chase?"

"Because he's a Nordic nutcase," said Greg. "This is his idea of a good time. Maybe if his mum had bought him an Xbox that would have kept him out of trouble."

"We must split up and block off as many routes as we can to make sure he doesn't get away," said Thor, laying a hand on his hammer. "Once we have him penned, I'll take care of the rest."

"You're right," Greg agreed. "As soon as somebody gets hold of him, shout out and we'll all come rushing."

"If we can find each other again," said Lewis.

"You should be a natural at this," said Greg. "You're always playing that Crabbyrinth game, the one with the giant crabs in the maze."

"I've not played that since I was seven," Lewis objected.

"It's like riding a bike, though," said Greg. "You don't forget how it's done."

"Good luck, boys," said Thor as they cautiously let go of each other and set out along separate paths.

Lewis carefully slid one foot forward then the other, all the while keeping one gloved hand pressed against the glassy wall of the maze. He was sure he had read that some mazes are easily solved, but he couldn't remember if you were meant to always take the left hand or the right hand path. And then he wasn't sure if that led you to the way out or to the centre.

As he was pondering this, he realised he had come to a dead end. The ice was so smooth he could make out a distorted reflection of his own face in it, staring back at him as if challenging him to solve the puzzle. Why had Loki gone to all the trouble of creating this maze in the first place?

He doubled back and took a left branch. There was a long stretch of path ahead of him now, so he moved carefully along it, hoping that it might lead somewhere.

He was halfway down the path when he heard the slap of running feet on the slick surface behind him. He caught the barest glimpse of a figure in a fur coat before the running man bashed him aside with his elbow and sent him sprawling across the ice.

Lewis lay there for a moment, cursing Loki and his tricks. Then he got onto his hands and knees and tried to stand.

"Get down, Lewis!" cried a voice.

It was Susie, racing towards him on her skates in pursuit of the fleeing man. She crouched forward for extra speed. Lewis dropped flat with a yelp as Susie leapt over him. The blades of her skates sliced the air above him, missing him by inches. She shot off down the passage and vanished round a corner.

From far off he heard Thor bellow and guessed that he'd been knocked flat too. Loki was leading them all on a merry chase, though why he was bothering to do it was a mystery.

The control Loki had over the winter weather allowed him to run across the ice without slipping while the rest of them floundered around as helpless as fish. It was then that Lewis recalled Loki wasn't the only one with a magical treasure. He reached into his pocket and pulled out the Ring Draupnir. Removing the glove from his left hand, he slipped the ring onto his middle finger.

All at once he knew – he just knew – the layout of the maze. It was as clear to him as if it were spread out on a computer screen. Actually, it wasn't especially complicated, with many paths criss-crossing each other and only a few dead ends. He supposed that Loki must have been wary of getting lost in it himself.

He was aware also of exactly where he was located, and everyone else as well. He could tell that Loki was bounding along confidently, never missing his footing on the ice. Susie was skating at high speed all around the maze searching for him. Thor was stomping along and falling flat on his face every third step. Greg was taking one tentative step after another while trying to look confident, as if anybody could see him.

Lewis began to move purposefully. He had a picture in his mind of an intersection where, if he timed it right, he would be able to intercept Loki as he passed.

He had a clear sense, almost like radar, that Loki was jogging down a passage to his right, on his way towards him. He tensed up all over and caught his breath as he reached the corner, ready to spring. He could hear the footfalls rushing closer, then there was his target, running past energetically as though out for a morning jog.

Lewis flung himself forward, but lost his footing and went sprawling. Clutching desperately, he managed to catch hold of the hem of Loki's fur coat as he went past. Clinging tightly, he was dragged along like a sledge being pulled by a team of huskies. Loki let out a wild laugh and hardly even slowed, so sure was his footing on the ice.

"I've got him!" Lewis shouted to the others.

They swerved this way and that around tight

bends, Lewis' legs whipping behind him. Gradually Loki began to slow and Lewis could hear him fighting for breath.

"Hang on, Lewis, I've got him in my sights!"

It was Susie's voice. Lewis looked up to see her racing towards him from the opposite direction. Loki skidded to a halt as she came flying at him on her skates and launched herself into the air. She threw herself at Loki, slamming him flat with Lewis trapped beneath.

"Susie, take it easy!" Lewis gasped.

"Sven! Greg! We've got him!" Susie yelled.

She kept Loki pinned down while Lewis wriggled out from beneath the prisoner.

There was an ear splitting crash as Thor smashed through the nearest ice wall with his hammer. Stepping over the frozen debris, he scowled down at his fellow god. "Now you pay the price for your misdeeds, Loki."

"You tell him, Sven," said Greg, stepping through the hole behind him.

The prisoner's fedora had slipped over his face so that all they could see of it was a tuft of red beard. Thor crushed the crown of the hat in his powerful fingers and lifted it up.

"By the beard of Odin!" he gasped when he saw the face beneath.

The beard had slipped askew and when Lewis gave it a tug it came away easily. "That's not Loki," he said.

"No," said Susie excitedly, "it's Garth Makepeace!"

9. THE ACTOR FACTOR

"Garth Makepeace!" Lewis echoed. "What are you doing here?"

"Makepeace?" said Thor. "Who is this Makepeace?"

"You've been out on the rigs too long," said Greg. "He's one of Hollywood's biggest stars."

"And me without my autograph book," said Susie, getting up off the actor. "Sorry about the knock, Mr Makepeace, but you shouldn't be running around in that disguise."

"Thanks for the tip, hotshot," Makepeace wheezed. "I've got to say, that was pretty fancy stunt work."

Lewis tossed the false beard aside and stared at the man on the ground. "If he's not Loki," he wondered out loud, "how was he able to run on the ice like that?"

"Because of these," growled Thor, grabbing Makepeace by the ankles and yanking up his feet. "The Shoes of Vidar. They have the power of surefootedness."

The shoes looked like plain moccasins with leather laces, not like any sort of treasure at all.

Makepeace caught his breath as Thor let his feet drop. "Larry told me he found them stashed away at the back of a shoe store," he said. "They sure do grip."

Thor seized him by the lapels of his coat and pulled him upright. "Makepeace, what are you doing here?" he demanded.

Makepeace chuckled. "Larry put me up to it. That guy is a riot! He makes cocktails you've never heard of. Have you ever tried a Red Rocket Root Beer?"

"Mr Makepeace, you're not explaining yourself very well," said Lewis.

"Call me Garth," said Makepeace good-naturedly.

He gently eased out of Thor's grip and smiled. "You see, Larry and I were playing cards for dares, and I lost. Again! So the dare was that I'd come here dressed as him and fool people for as long as I could. I think my performance was pretty hot," he added. "Worth a Golden Globe at least. Too bad I couldn't keep it up, but I wasn't expecting anybody to show up in skates."

"How did you get here?" asked Susie.

"In my limo," answered Makepeace. "My driver slipped and twisted his ankle, so we left him behind and Larry drove."

"What, through all this snow?" said Lewis.

"It was a crazy ride!" Makepeace enthused. "The snow opened up in front of us like it was being held back by the cops. That Larry, he must be some kind of special effects wizard."

"Something like that," said Greg.

"Hand over the shoes, Makepeace," Thor commanded, extending his hand. "They are the property of Asgard."

"Sure," said Makepeace, slipping the shoes off and handing them over. "No need to get sore. Good thing I brought a pair of designer loafers with me." From an inside pocket of his coat he pulled out a pair of expensive Italian shoes and slipped them on. "Now *these* have style," he beamed.

Thor tucked the Shoes of Vidar into his belt. "So Loki was never here," he said. "It was all some sort of a trick."

"Yeah, what a goof!" Makepeace laughed. "Who are you guys, anyway?"

"We're Lewis and Greg McBride," said Lewis. "You played golf with our dad."

"Say, that's right," said Makepeace. "Al McBride. He wanted me to sign up for some pro-am celebrity tournament in October."

"This is Susie," said Greg. "And this is Sven. You could say he and Larry are cousins."

"Larry's the black sheep of the family," Thor added grimly.

Makepeace cast an interested eye over him. "You

know, pal, you look like you really work out. Have you ever thought of hiring yourself out as a personal trainer?"

Thor ignored him and swung Mjolnir from side to side, scanning the area. "There are definitely no other treasures around here," he said.

Makepeace picked up the fedora Thor had discarded and clamped it on his head. "Say, could we go some place warmer? It's like sitting inside a freezer here."

"It's a long way back to your hotel, Mr Makepeace," said Lewis.

"No problem," said Makepeace. "My limo's heated and it's parked right around the corner."

"A limo," said Susie. "Cool!"

"We still have to find a way out of this maze," Greg pointed out.

"I've got that covered," said Lewis. He took off his glove and displayed the ring.

"The data ring," said Susie. "So that's how you zeroed in on Garth."

Guided by the ring, Lewis led them all out of the football ground. By then his head was throbbing with the knowledge being fed into it. Once they were out in the street, he took the ring off and put it back in his pocket.

"So you guys and Larry are all buddies, right?" said Makepeace. "That's why he's joking around with you."

"He is our bitter foe," growled Thor, brandishing a clenched fist, "as are any who align with him."

"Hey, it was just a bit of fun," said the actor, raising his hands defensively. "No need to start a war over it."

As Makepeace had said, there was a long silver car parked around the corner. Makepeace took out the key and pushed a button to unlock the doors. They had to dig away some of the snow before they could open them and get inside. Makepeace took the driver's seat with Thor on the passenger side, while Greg, Lewis and Susie climbed in behind them.

"It's as big as a bus in here!" Susie declared.

The floor was covered in plush carpeting and there was a state of the art entertainment system with a TV screen and speakers. Makepeace flicked on the heat and soon it was warm enough for everybody to take off their hats.

"I've got a flask of hot coffee here," said Makepeace, opening the glove compartment. "Just pass it around."

The coffee was so strong and sweet Lewis could hardly swallow it, but Greg and Susie took a couple of big gulps each.

"I can't get my head around this," said Greg, handing back the flask. "Why would Loki send this guy here instead of coming himself?"

"He wouldn't," said Lewis, "if there was a treasure hidden here. But there isn't."

"Then what has all this running about been in aid of?" Susie wondered.

Thor laid a fist on the dashboard. "Makepeace, what do you know about this?"

"It's like I said," the star answered. "Larry wanted me to lead you on a chase. Like that scene in my movie *Danger Agent*, where I lead the killers down through the Paris sewers. We filmed that in a real sewer, you know. I was taking showers for a week."

"So Loki wanted to keep us occupied," said Lewis, "while he was somewhere else."

"But where?" said Susie. "And why?"

"Look, Sven says there's a whole load of these treasures," said Greg. "It's bound to take Loki at least a couple of days to track them all down. So what good does it do him to have us tied up here for an hour or two?"

"Maybe he's not after them all," said Lewis.

"What do you mean?" said Thor, raising an eyebrow.

"Well, it seems to me that he wasn't that bothered about hanging on to the ring. He acted more like he wanted to get out of the cathedral and go somewhere else."

"I think Lewis is on to something," said Greg. "Suppose Loki doesn't want all the treasures. Suppose there's only one he's really trying to find."

"Ja, that could be right," said Thor, rubbing his beard thoughtfully.

"Sven, is one of the treasures more important than the others?" Lewis asked.

Thor frowned. "That's hard to say. They're all so different from each other."

"What are you guys talking about?" Makepeace interrupted. "Is it some kind of movie script, like *Searchers Of The Lost Temple*?"

"Quiet, Makepeace!" Thor ordered.

The star went back to drinking his coffee in silence.

"Let's think it through logically," said Lewis. "What does Loki want more than anything else?"

"To annoy everybody and cause trouble?" Greg suggested.

"More than that," said Lewis. "Last time we ran into him, he'd conjured up a special day that gave him all his godlike powers back, and he was planning to make it last forever."

"Well, he can't do that again," said Greg. "We saw to that."

"But is there another way he could regain the powers of a god?" Lewis persisted.

"Not even with all the treasures could he do that," said Thor. "And in time the powers of the treasures again will fade."

"So how could he get back to being a god?" asked Lewis.

"To do that," said Thor, "he'd have to return to Asgard. But that is impossible since the Bifrost was destroyed. Without the Bifrost connecting Asgard to Earth, we are all cut off from the source of our power."

"So is there any way one of the treasures could help him get back to Asgard?" asked Lewis.

"What about the shoes?" said Greg. "Could he walk there if he had them?"

"He already gave the shoes away to Garth here," said Susie, "so that can't be it."

"Sven, is there anything else that could connect Asgard and Earth?" Lewis asked.

"There used to be the world tree, the Yggdrasil," said Thor. "That connected the Nine Realms of the Universe, but it was destroyed centuries ago by the frost giants."

"Hey!" Greg exclaimed. "Didn't you say one of the treasures was some kind of seed?"

Thor's eyes grew wide. "Ja, the Yggdrasil Seed. Gotterdamerung! That's it, guys!"

"What is this seed, Sven?" asked Susie. "Some sort of GM crop?"

"The seed is all that is left of the world tree after it was destroyed," said Thor.

"Do you suppose Loki could use it to grow a new Yggdrasil tree?" Lewis wondered.

"You may be on to something," Thor said. "And if he used it to reach Asgard..." His voice tailed off and his eyes became gloomy.

"Yes, what?" Lewis prompted him.

Thor drew a deep breath. "Then he could sit upon the throne of Odin and be master of Asgard."

"That doesn't sound good," said Susie.

"It sure isn't good, Susie," said Thor. "With the power of Asgard at his command, that villain could destroy all us other gods... and the Earth as well."

10. PEOPLE IN GLASS HOUSES

"You mean he'd bring on Ragnarok," Lewis gasped, "the end of the world!"

Makepeace choked on his coffee. "End of the world? What kind of a picture are you guys cooking up?"

"Hang on," said Greg. "A tree takes years to grow, so this Iggy-dross world tree must take even longer."

"Not if it's been genetically modified," said Susie. "You should pay more attention to the news."

"These magical things don't follow the normal rules," said Lewis. "Remember Lokiday? And look at how fast this winter weather came on."

"So is Loki going to keep bouncing around town till he finds the seed?" asked Greg.

"If that was the case, there would be no point luring us out here," said Lewis. "He must have worked out how to get the one treasure he's been searching for all along, and he wanted us nowhere near it."

Susie leaned forward over the back of the passenger

seat. "How about it, Sven? Can you tell which treasure is which when you detect them?"

"No," answered Thor. "I just get a fix on the general area they are in."

"Maybe there's a logic to it," suggested Lewis. "Remember Loki told us he found the ring under the gravestone of a man named Bell?"

"And the shoes were in a shoe shop, right, Mr Makepeace?" said Susie.

"Right," the actor agreed.

"And the hammer was in our garage among the tools," said Greg. "But what about the winter box? Why was that under the Swilken Bridge?"

"Loki said the Troll King made it for him," said Lewis, "and in the old stories, trolls live under bridges."

"Like in the Three Billy Goats Gruff," said Susie. "You're right, Lewis, there's a pattern to it."

"So where would the seed be?" Greg wondered.

Thor thumped his fist on the steering wheel in front of the actor. "Makepeace, what else did Loki say to you?"

The actor blinked. "You mean Larry? Not much. When he left me here, he said he was going to the only place in town that's warm all year round. I guess he was going to a sauna."

"A sauna?" said Greg. "That doesn't make any sense."

"He wasn't talking about a sauna," said Lewis

excitedly. "There's another place that's kept warm all year round. The Botanic Gardens."

"What's so warm about a garden?" said Greg.

"Oh right, you've never been there, have you?"

"And why would I want to wander around looking at plants, Lewis? I'm not a farmer."

"They have a lot of tropical plants there," said Susie. "They keep them in glasshouses that are always warm."

"It sounds like the perfect place for the Yggdrasil Seed," said Lewis.

"I think you've hit the nail on the head," said Thor. "Where are these gardens?"

"They're right across town," said Greg. "Loki made sure to lure us in the wrong direction."

"We can show you the way," said Susie.

"What are you guys up to?" said Garth Makepeace, sounding bemused. "It sounds like some kind of scavenger hunt."

"Mr Makepeace..." Lewis began.

"Call me Garth."

"Garth, you should try to get back to your hotel."

"Are you kidding?" exclaimed the actor. "I was bored out of my skull back there. Why else do you think I played along with this gag of Larry's?"

"We are on a dangerous quest, Makepeace," said Thor. "It is no place for a play actor."

"You don't need to worry about me," said Makepeace. "Not as long as I've got this." He reached into his pocket and pulled out a small golden object.

Thor squinted at it. "A cigarette lighter?"

"It's my lucky lighter," said Makepeace. "Back home in Missouri my old man gave it to me when I was fifteen. 'Son,' he told me, 'the discovery of fire was the beginning of human civilisation. As long as you can make fire, you'll never be out of luck.'"

He pressed the switch and a small flame sprang from the lighter. "I've been carrying it around ever since and you know what? He was right. I've been one lucky guy."

He snapped the lighter shut and slipped it back in his pocket.

"It's going to be easier just to let him tag along," said Greg.

Lewis nodded resignedly.

"All right then," Thor agreed. "But try to stay out of our way."

"You won't even know I'm there," Makepeace promised. "I'll be like the Invisible Man, you know, in that old movie."

"We only have four pairs of skis," Susie pointed out.

"Makepeace can share mine," said Thor. "I'll have to keep an eye on him anyway."

As soon as they left the warmth of the car, the cold air hit them like the slap of an icy hand.

"I sure am glad I've got this coat," said Makepeace, flapping his arms to stay warm. "It's like *Ice Station Zebra* out here."

When the others had fastened on their skis, Thor said, "You get behind me, Makepeace, with your feet on the skis. Hang on tight to my belt and don't let go."

Makepeace followed the instructions with a perplexed expression. "It'll take forever waddling all the way across town on these things."

"Not as long as you think," said Greg. "Okay, Sven, fire them up."

Thor held Mjolnir aloft and the skis immediately started moving.

"Yeehoo!" exclaimed Makepeace. "That's some trick, Sven. Have these things got motors in them or what?"

"Quiet, Makepeace, or I'll make you walk," Thor growled.

"Got you," the actor acknowledged.

They gathered speed, racing along Lamond Drive. Even if anyone had been out in the street to spot them, they were virtually invisible amidst the snow flurries. Lewis directed Thor along Broomfaulds Avenue and down the Canongate until they pulled up at the entrance to the Botanic Gardens. There was no snow falling on the car park and the path beyond the gate had been swept clear.

"Loki's made it easy for himself to get around," said Greg, "and for us, too."

"He thinks we're at the other end of town sliding around his ice maze," said Lewis. "He didn't think we'd catch Garth Makepeace as fast as we did."

As everybody took off their skis, Thor said, "Carry them with you. We might need them."

"Too true," said Greg, recalling their battle with the ice serpent.

With their skis under their arms, they walked past the empty wooden gatehouse and gift shop.

"The place looks deserted," said Susie.

"I expect the staff headed home before they got snowed in," said Lewis.

As they passed the tea hut on their right, Makepeace peered through the frosted window. "Say, there's a coffee machine in there. What do you say we stop for a hot drink?"

"We will toast our victory later," said Thor, striding on.

The snow was piled in heaps on both sides of the path. The tall trees that loomed above them were draped in white, like enormous ghosts. Wooden signs poked out of the snow. Beyond the frozen waste of the Peace Garden they saw the glasshouses. There was a whole row of them linked together by a long corridor, forming a network of controlled environments for exotic plants from all around the world. The glass walls were clouded with condensation. It was impossible to tell if there was anybody inside.

"We're too exposed out here," said Thor, dropping into a crouch. "We must get inside and use the plants for cover."

The others hunched down beside him.

"Loki might not even be here," said Greg. "He might already have found the seed and bolted."

"No," said Thor. "If he was gone, it would be snowing here. He's keeping the place clear until he gets what he's after."

Lewis led the way to the main entrance and they stacked their skis outside the door. A sign said Temperate Corridor.

"Stay behind me," Thor instructed, "and keep quiet. Taking him by surprise, that is our best chance."

"Not much chance of that," said Greg. "All the walls are made of glass."

"Just keep low," said Thor.

They passed quietly into a small entrance hall, then through a second door that led into the Temperate Corridor. The first stretch was marked Cool Temperate and was lined with tall green plants.

To their right was a glass door marked Desert House. Peering in, Lewis saw a long room filled with different kinds of cactus. Some were tall and spindly with needles protruding in all directions; some were thick and squat, though their spines looked just as sharp. Others were just huge clusters of thick, spiky leaves.

"Now this *does* look like an alien planet," Susie murmured.

"No sign of Loki, though," said Lewis.

The next door led to the Alpine House. This featured an aisle of sandstone paving with short, scrubby plants clustered round rocks on both sides. In contrast to the Desert House, it looked tame and domestic.

"There's definitely nobody in there," said Greg. "You couldn't hide a mouse in those shrubs."

Another door marked Warm Temperate led to the next section of the corridor. Here the air was warmer and the plants more lush and colourful. The signs marked out olives, oleander and acanthus. There were two more glasshouses on the right, but there was no one in there either.

The door leading into the last stretch of corridor was marked Tropical. Here the air was stiflingly hot and moist. This area housed coffee, banana and papaya plants. The first door on the right was marked Display

House. As soon as he glanced through the glass, Lewis hissed, "There he is!"

Everyone crouched low among the exotic foliage and watched the figure moving at the far end of the glasshouse. There was no mistake this time. It was Loki.

Makepeace craned his neck for a better look. "Say, that's a Montague Burton tweed overcoat he's wearing. I love those!"

"Down!" Thor commanded, grabbing the actor by the shoulder and forcing him to his knees. "Keep still, and keep quiet!"

Peeking through a screen of fronds, Lewis saw that Loki was standing in the midst of some potted plants and poster displays. He was gleefully tossing what looked like a large nut up and down in his hand.

"I think he's found the Yggdrasil Seed," said Lewis.

Thor's broad face hardened. "Then we must take it from him by force."

"Hold on a second," Lewis cautioned him. "Last time we tackled him head on, he nearly buried us in an avalanche."

"You're right, Lewis," said Greg. "We need to try something different this time."

"How about Garth?" Susie suggested.

"What do you mean, Spinny?" asked Greg.

"Loki doesn't know that Garth is on our side now," Susie pointed out. "Maybe we can trick him."

Lewis saw what she was getting at. "That's right!" he exclaimed. "With a bit of luck, Garth could get close enough to snatch the seed."

"How about it, Garth?" asked Greg. "Are you game?"

Makepeace looked uneasy. "I can't say I feel good about it. Larry and I are buds, you know. Are you sure he's out to destroy the universe?"

"Yes, we're sure, Makepeace," Thor insisted forcefully. "Now are you part of the solution or part of the problem?"

Makepeace squared his shoulders. "Hey, I'm with you guys." He grinned. "I've saved the world a dozen times in my movies but I never thought I'd get to do it for real."

"You need to con him into thinking you shook us off," said Lewis. "And that you guessed he was coming here."

"Don't let on that you know who he really is," Greg added.

"Relax," said Makepeace. "I won an MTV award, you know. I can pull this off in my sleep."

"You only have to keep it up long enough to grab the seed, then get back here fast," said Greg.

"I'll take care of the rest," said Thor.

While the others crouched low in cover, Makepeace

stood up and smoothed his hair. He opened the door and strolled down the length of the glasshouse as casually as if he were walking into a coffee shop.

Loki looked up in surprise, clenching the seed tightly in his fist. He asked a question in too low a voice for Lewis and the others to hear, but they could see Makepeace smiling and making friendly gestures. They could tell he had launched into a story about how he'd shaken off Thor and his friends. Loki laughed, and resumed tossing the seed up and down in the air.

Greg gave Lewis' sleeve a tug. "I don't get it. Why does he keep looking at Garth's feet?"

Lewis' heart skipped a beat. They had made a big mistake. "Oh no! We should have thought of that," he groaned.

Loki raised a quizzical eyebrow as Makepeace pulled out a large wallet and talked excitedly. A few more words passed between them, then Loki tossed something right at the actor. Makepeace plucked it out of the air, turned and ran.

The door flew open as he rushed into the Tropical Corridor where the others stood up to congratulate him. "I got the seed!" he declared triumphantly, brandishing his clenched fist. "Let's vamoose!"

Lewis was seized by a sudden doubt. "But how did you get it away from him?" he asked.

"A piece of cake!" laughed Makepeace. "I bet him a thousand bucks I could tell him what plant that nut came from, and he just tossed it to me. See?"

He opened his hand to display his prize.

Thor scowled. "Makepeace, that is not the Yggdrasil Seed."

Makepeace was stunned. "It's not?"

"No," said Lewis, taking the object from the actor's palm. "It's just a pebble."

"He pulled a switcheroo on me!" Makepeace gasped. "But why?"

"Didn't you notice how he was looking at your shoes?" asked Lewis.

"Everybody looks at my shoes," said Makepeace. "I told you, they're designer."

"But they're not the Shoes of Vidar," said Lewis.

Thor nodded sombrely. "And if you're not wearing the Shoes of Vidar, how did you get across town so fast through all this snow?"

"Yes, you should have thought of that sooner," said a mocking voice from behind them. Loki was leaning against the doorway with the seed between his thumb and forefinger. "There's a display about ash trees down there," he continued smugly, "and as some of you might know, the Yggdrasil is a kind of ash."

"Thanks for the botany lesson, Loki," said Greg.

"What are you going to do now? Open a garden centre?"

Loki bared his teeth unpleasantly. "The first thing I'm going to do is get rid of you meddling idiots for once and for all."

"Whoa, Larry, there's no need to get all steamed up," Makepeace protested mildly.

"I'm disappointed in you, Garth," Loki frowned, "taking sides with these losers after all the good times we've had."

Makepeace laughed unconvincingly. "Hey, Larry, I was just kidding around, you know."

"Two things you should never do, my friends," said Loki. "Never steal a banana from a gorilla and never try to trick the god of mischief."

"*Enough!*" shouted Thor. He strode forward, muscular hands clutching Mjolnir with warlike intent. "No more games, Loki. No more ice monsters. Just you and me."

"The trouble with you," sneered Loki, "is you don't have much imagination. You see, the Yggdrasil Seed has special powers too."

Clutching the seed firmly in one hand, he snapped his fingers. As if in answer to his command, the surrounding plants stiffened like soldiers standing to attention. When Loki waved his hand they ripped their roots out of the ground and launched themselves at Thor.

Thor tried to beat them aside with Mjolnir, but they shot right past the hammer. Two plants whipped themselves around his arms like handcuffs while others piled on top of him and dragged him down like an angry mob. Greg and Lewis waded in to help him, only to be engulfed in the frenzied, thrashing greenery.

11. MONEY TO BURN

"This is the worst thing yet!" Greg exclaimed. "It's like we're drowning in jungle." He ducked as a seed pod the size of a football swung at him, just missing his head.

A leaf as big as a deck chair slammed Lewis in the back. Winded, he gasped, "Hey, the plants weren't this big when we came in!"

"Loki's using that seed to make them bigger," puffed Greg. He broke off with a grunt as an oversized shrub butted him in the chest.

Roots reared up off the floor like snakes to entangle their legs while branches lashed at them from above. Greg caught hold of a flailing frond and tried to twist it apart, but it was like wrestling with a huge rubber band. Holding it at bay with one hand, he used the other to pull out his Swiss army knife. He popped open the cutting blade and hacked at the stem.

"This is no use," he panted. "It'd take an axe to whack this thing."

The tangle of branches pressed tighter, blocking

out the light. Lewis was bracing himself to go under when suddenly a rip appeared in the wall of vegetation.

There came a sound of slashing and tearing and shreds of vegetation went flying in all directions. Through the widening gap Lewis caught sight of Susie.

She had the blades from her skates, one in each hand, and was using them to slice her way through the choking greenery. When she reached the brothers she demanded breathlessly, "Where are Sven and Garth?"

"I don't know," Lewis answered, tugging at a frond that was wrapping itself around his throat. "I can't see anything for all these leaves."

"This is ridiculous," Susie seethed. "They're growing back as fast as I cut them."

"That's because of the magic," said Greg as he wrestled an enormous fern.

"Gutters!" said Susie, chopping through a tangle of fronds. "It's genetic mutation, that's all."

Suddenly Thor burst through the foliage like a stampeding rhino, torn vines trailing from his arms. He waded towards them, chopping to his left and right with Mjolnir, but the tangle of branches simply took the blows and sprang back.

"A hammer's not the best thing for fighting plants, is it?" said Susie.

"Ja, I'd give a lot for a good sword right now," said Thor, bashing at the trunk of a banana plant.

The four of them drew together back to back, struggling to fight off the greenery that threatened to smother them. Greg's knife went flying as a lashing vine smacked it from his hand. Susie lost one of her skates and did her best to fight on with the other. Lewis punched and kicked as hard as he could, but twin clusters of overgrown papaya leaves got hold of him like monstrous hands and began to squeeze the breath out of him.

Out of nowhere came a sudden whiff of smoke and a flash of flame. A bundle of burning paper dropped into the midst of the struggle and the plants recoiled at once, snatching their branches out of harm's way.

As the leaves parted, Lewis spotted Garth Makepeace calmly setting fire to bundles of money with his lighter and tossing them at the rampaging vegetation. The green horrors jerked back and retreated from the flames like mice running from a cat.

"Wow, that's some save, Garth!" Susie enthused, shaking off a scattering of seeds.

"Did you never see that old movie *Attack of the Killer*

Creepers?" the actor asked with a grin. "Giant man-eating plants hate fire. See?"

He lit another bundle of notes and flung it at the plants.

"Those are hundred-pound notes!" Lewis exclaimed as Makepeace joined them.

"So what?" said the actor. "It's only money."

Thor looked around and grimaced. "Did you see which way Loki went?"

Makepeace shook his head. "We'd better not stick around here much longer," he warned. "I only carry so much cash on me."

"We must get back to the skis," said Thor.

"Okay, this is the last bundle," said Makepeace, lighting a handful of notes. Thrusting it ahead of him, he forced a path through the greenery. Angry walls of shrubbery loomed on either hand, but the plants kept their distance.

The paper burned quickly. They were almost at the threshold when Makepeace uttered a yelp of pain and let the last fiery fragment fall. Thor lunged forward and threw open the door. "Go!" he shouted.

Once he had bundled everybody through, Thor dived in after them, slamming the door behind him. A wave of dense greenery smacked up against the glass and fell back, limbs thrashing in frustration.

In the corridor beyond, a new threat awaited them. Lewis skidded to a halt with a cry of dismay.

A gang of enormous cacti, swollen to horrendous size, had burst out of the Desert Room and invaded the corridor. Bristling like a nest of bayonets, they barred the way back to the entrance.

Greg threw up his arms. "Oh come on! Ice monsters are one thing, but giant cactuses are right over the score!"

Lewis swallowed hard. "Actually the plural of cactus is *cacti*."

"It doesn't matter what you call them, Lewis – they don't have any ears!" Greg retorted.

The cactus plants were edging forward, their spikes swishing the air.

"Quick! The other way!" ordered Thor.

As they wheeled around, the glass wall to their right gave way and a towering row of grotesque shapes lumbered out in front of them. What looked like enormous snapping mouths mounted on rubbery tendrils lunged at them hungrily. A memory of one of his biology classes told Lewis what they were.

"Venus flytraps!" he shouted to the others. "They're carnivores! If they catch you, they'll eat you!"

The huge flytraps shuffled forward, their jaws gaping, and a sickly sweet fragrance filled the air.

"I think we're trapped, all right," said Makepeace.

"Maybe not!" exclaimed Susie.

Beckoning frantically, she pointed to a set of double doors in an alcove to their left. They were marked PRIVATE. Greg tugged at the handle.

"It's no good, they're locked!" he shouted.

"Stand aside!" growled Thor, raising his hammer.

With one mighty blow he dashed the lock to pieces and kicked the doors open. Beyond lay a storeroom with clay pots, bags of fertiliser, and garden tools stacked up against the walls. There was a door at the far end. Thor pointed the way with Mjolnir. "Run!" he shouted.

Makepeace and Greg rushed the far door and threw their shoulders against it. It gave way and they tumbled out onto the snow-covered ground with Lewis and Susie on their heels. As Thor ran after them, one of the flytraps lashed out and caught hold of his leg. It snatched him up and shook him like a doll.

Thor twisted in the air and lashed out with Mjolnir. The hammer connected with the plant's lower jaw and a jet of sap burst out. The flytrap went mad, bashing the god of thunder against the roof, then slamming him to the floor.

The others rushed back to help as the vicious plant whipped Thor this way and that, but more hungry mouths came snapping at them. Lewis stepped back outside and scooped up a big handful of snow.

"Take that!" he yelled, flinging it at one of the plant monsters.

The Venus flytrap shrivelled at the freezing impact and recoiled.

"Hey, that's a good idea!" Greg exclaimed.

He and Susie joined Lewis in bombarding the plants with snowballs until they dropped Thor.

"They're tropical plants!" said Lewis triumphantly. "They can't stand the snow."

"You guys keep up the attack," Makepeace told them. "I'll get Sven out of there."

He scrambled across the storeroom floor and grabbed Thor by the arm. As the rain of snowballs kept the flytraps at bay, he hauled their stricken friend outside and slammed the door shut. Thor was badly bruised, and had a nasty-looking gash on the side of his head, but he was still clinging to Mjolnir.

"Boy, that was like one of those old war movies," said Makepeace, "where the sergeant has to rescue one of his men from under fire. I always wanted to be in one of those."

Lewis and Greg tried to get Thor back on his feet, but his right leg gave out from under him and he sank to the ground with a grimace of pain. "I can't make it," he moaned. "You had best get away and leave me for the wolves."

"There aren't any wolves in St Andrews," said Lewis.

"And we're not leaving you," added Greg.

"This will be tough going if he can't walk," said Makepeace.

"Take care of Sven while I go get the skis," said Susie, dashing off around the corner. She reappeared moments later, her face pale. "Sorry, guys, the skis are gone," she reported miserably. "I made a dive for them, but a bunch of cactuses scooped them up and snatched them inside."

"That's that, then," said Greg. "If we go back in there, they'll chew us up and use us for compost."

"We'll just have to manage without the skis," said Lewis.

Susie cast an anxious glance at Thor. "Do you think it's okay to move him?"

"We'll freeze to death if we stay here," said Greg.

Makepeace gave Thor's shoulder a gentle shake. "Hey, big guy, can you hear me? We need to make tracks."

Thor stirred and groaned. "I hear you. Help me up."

With Thor's arms wrapped around their shoulders, Makepeace and Greg managed to get him moving. A fresh fall of snow filled the air with thick white flakes.

"Come on! The car park's this way," urged Lewis.

He and Susie took the lead while Greg and Makepeace supported Thor behind them. By the time they reached the entrance to the gardens, the blizzard was so intense they could barely see more than a few yards in any direction.

They struggled across the car park, their feet numbed by the deep snow. Thor was doing his best to stay upright, but he was clearly approaching the end of his strength.

"I feel like I'm turning into a popsicle," said Makepeace. "Between the plants and the snow, Larry's sure put us in a bind."

"Loki's cranked up the freezer," said Greg through chattering teeth.

"He wants to finish us off," said Lewis, as they emerged into the Canongate Road, "so we can't cause him any more trouble."

His left foot went from under him and he fell. Greg and Makepeace tripped over him and went down, taking Thor with them. The god of thunder struggled to rise, then collapsed on his back. "My leg is wrecked," he muttered weakly. "In the old days I would have shrugged this off like nothing, but now..."

His voice trailed off into a stream of unhappy Norse mutterings.

"This isn't good," said Susie, her voice shaking as she dropped to her knees. She looked completely exhausted.

Lewis pulled out his phone and tried to call his parents, but, as before, the extreme weather had brought the network down and there was no signal. Lewis' heart sank. He felt frozen right through and didn't see how they could make it any further. The snow was falling faster than ever, and if they didn't get out of here, it wouldn't be long before they were buried.

Greg's eye suddenly lighted on the Shoes of Vidar, which were still tucked into Thor's belt. He grabbed them and said, "That's the stuff!"

The energy in his voice jolted Lewis out of his stupor. He watched, shivering, as Greg swapped the magic shoes for his boots. Tying the laces of the boots together, he slung them over his shoulder and took a few experimental steps. He found he could walk over the surface of the snow as easily as if it were solid.

"Hey, these are really comfy," he said. "They feel like the best trainers ever."

"I'll bet they're no Skyliners," Susie joked, forcing her frozen lips into a smile.

"You guys take care of Sven," Greg instructed. "I'll run on ahead and get help."

Setting off at a jog, he disappeared into the blizzard.

"I hope he doesn't get lost," Lewis groaned.

Susie pressed up next to him, shoulder to shoulder. "We've got the lights on at home," she reminded him. "He's bound to spot those."

"I wouldn't count on it."

Susie gave him a poke in the arm. "You know, Lewis, if Greg spent as much time worrying as you do, neither of you would ever get anything done. Of course, if you both barged ahead without thinking the way he does, you'd probably fall over a cliff."

"Hanging around with him is a lot like walking along the edge of a cliff," Lewis agreed.

"He is kind of a goof, isn't he?" Susie chuckled.

"Is that why you like him?"

"He makes me laugh, right enough, but that's not all of it. You see, Lewis, Greg doesn't worry about the problems other people get hung up on. Now, I've scored a lot of goals, and you can't do that if you're scared to take on the defence. Greg's not scared to take on the defence."

"The shoes will guide him," muttered Thor, propping himself up on one elbow. Even that effort seemed to cause him further agony. "That is their power."

Garth Makepeace leaned over him, trying to protect Thor from the worst of the blizzard. "You know, this reminds me of a movie I did once where I was trapped on an iceberg," the actor recalled.

"Right now, that doesn't sound so bad," said Lewis, pulling his hood tightly around his face.

"It was worse than you think. There was a bomb inside the ice, set to explode in ten minutes."

"So how did you escape?" Susie asked.

"Darned if I can remember," said Makepeace. "I had a beautiful lady scientist with me and she did most of the hard work."

"Women usually do," said Susie.

Thor stirred feebly. "You know, Makepeace, you're not such a bad guy," he murmured, "for a play actor..." His voice tailed off and his eyes closed.

Susie bowed her head and hugged herself tightly against the cold. She mumbled, "I don't suppose anybody's got a bar of chocolate on them?"

Lewis shook his head numbly.

"That would be worth about a million bucks right now, wouldn't it?" grunted Makepeace.

Lewis gazed down at Thor. The Norse god's face was pale and flecked with snow and there was a frozen ribbon of blood on his cheek. If not for the rising and falling of his broad chest, it would be impossible to tell that he was still alive.

Lewis wished he knew how long Greg had been

gone, but the effort of looking at his watch would use more energy than he had left. All they could do was huddle close to Thor, doing their best to shelter him.

And the snow kept on falling.

12. SPAGHETTI AND MEATBALLS

"What's that?" Susie croaked suddenly.

Lewis realised his eyes had drooped shut and he had to rub the ice from his lashes before he could open them. The air all around was a blur of white. He tried to say 'where?' but it came out as 'ungh'.

"Have my eyes gone screwy," he heard Garth Makepeace murmur, "or are those lights coming our way?"

A torch flared out of the gloom and Greg appeared behind it, trotting along in the Shoes of Vidar. Racing up to them, he wheeled in his tracks and jumped up and down, waving. "Here they are!"

Dad and Mr Spinetti appeared through the curtain of snow, dragging a sledge behind them. They were dressed in arctic gear with thermal gloves and goggles.

"Come on," said Dad, pulling Lewis to his feet, "you need to get moving before you freeze solid."

Greg and Mr Spinetti hauled Susie and Makepeace to their feet, then cleared the snow from Thor, who had almost disappeared under a blanket of white. Dad passed around a flask of hot minestrone soup. After a couple of gulps Lewis felt a welcome glow inside.

"Yum! My favourite!" said Susie, with a lively gleam returning to her eye.

Mr Spinetti propped up Thor's head and forced some brandy between his lips. "There you go, get that down you."

As he swallowed, Thor's eyes flickered open and he gazed around him groggily. "For a moment," he groaned, "I thought the Valkyries had come to take my soul to Valhalla."

"It's not come to that yet," said Dad.

Mr Spinetti passed out heated thermal packs, which they tucked inside their coats. Their warmth brought an immediate relief. Between the thermal packs and the soup, Lewis felt like he was coming out of a coma.

"I don't know about you, Lewis," said Greg, flapping his arms, "but I don't think I'm going to build another snowman as long as I live."

"This blizzard's getting worse," said Mr Spinetti, "so we need to be on our way. Come on!"

With Dad's help, he picked Thor up and laid him gently on the sledge. Once Thor was securely wrapped in warm blankets, they set off up the road, hauling the sledge behind them.

"I wish that chap who's always dreaming of a white Christmas was here now," said Dad. "I bet this would change his mind."

"Al, this isn't some trick of yours to make me stick around for your golf tournament, is it?" Makepeace joked.

"If it doesn't work, we can always get Johnny Depp instead," said Dad.

Makepeace wagged a finger at him. "Never settle for second best, Al, never settle for second best."

When at last they came in sight of the Christmas lights decorating the Spinetti house, Lewis had never been so glad to see anything in his life. Once they were inside, Dad and Mr Spinetti took Thor to one of the bedrooms where they got him into warm, dry pyjamas and put him under an electric blanket. Lewis and Greg's mum was a nurse, so she cleaned and bandaged the cut on his head and gave him some painkillers.

Once she was done, she joined the rest of the company in the front room where Garth Makepeace was being introduced to everyone as he warmed himself by the gas fire. Susie's brothers Michael and Charlie were running around the room making noises like fighter planes.

"Do you mind telling us what you've been up to out there?" asked Mr McBride, tapping his empty pipe against his lower lip. "You look like you've been through the wars."

"It's a bit of a long story," Lewis mumbled, knowing how impossible it would all sound.

"It's top secret actually," said Greg. "You know, like in a spy film."

"It's like a movie, all right," Makepeace agreed.

"We really need Sven here to explain it properly," said Susie.

"Well, I suppose it can wait till he's rested up a bit," said Mrs McBride.

Charlie dived between Makepeace's legs and rolled across the carpet, making machine gun noises.

"I think they've seen my movie *Ace of Wings* one too many times," said the actor with a twinkle in his eye.

"I was just watching one of your films last week," said Mum, "the romantic one where you're chasing after that girl in Geneva."

"*Swiss Kiss*," said Makepeace. "Yeah, that's one of my favourites. Did you know we spent three days filming that scene where we dance in the fountain?"

"I remember watching you years ago in that teenage TV show *Atlantis High Adventures*," said Mrs Spinetti.

"Whoa there, Theresa!" said Makepeace. "Don't start dragging out my baby pictures."

"Now don't ruin your appetite," said Mum, noticing how they were all guzzling digestive biscuits and custard creams. "Theresa and I have whipped up a big dinner for everybody."

"It's not turkey and Christmas pudding, is it?" laughed Susie.

"We couldn't quite manage that," said her mother, "but I don't think you'll be disappointed."

Once the table was laid they all sat down while Mr and Mrs Spinetti ferried dishes of spaghetti and meatballs out of the kitchen, all of it in a delicious-smelling sauce.

Thor limped in, leaning on a crutch made from an old mop handle. Every move he made appeared to hurt him, much as he tried to hide it, but he refused all offers of help.

"The smell of that food is all I need to get me to the table," he joked.

Mrs Spinetti said a blessing over the meal, then everybody tucked in. Soon their plates were piled high with spaghetti and meatballs and garlic bread. Thor and Garth Makepeace joined Dad and Mr Spinetti in having a glass of home brew.

"Say, you should go into business with this stuff,

George," said Makepeace, smacking his lips. "It really hits the spot."

"It is worthy to be drunk in Valhalla," Thor agreed, draining his glass.

"Easy there, Sven," Dad cautioned him. "It can go straight to your head. Especially on top of those painkillers."

"Don't worry about me," said Thor, giving him a wink. "I grew up drinking mead that would flatten a troll."

Mr Spinetti laid his fork aside and eyed the youngsters. "Now that we're all here, do you not think it's about time you told us what you've been up to all day?"

Lewis cleared his throat nervously. "Well, it's kind of complicated."

"That's right," said Susie. "It's hard to know where to begin."

"Stolen antiquities," Greg declared loudly.

Dad stared at him. "Antiquities?"

"The guy who calls himself Larry O'Keefe is really an international art thief." Greg was chewing on a meatball and swallowed it before carrying on. "He stole a lot of valuable antiquities from the National Museum of Scandivaria."

Lewis groaned inwardly. He wished there was some way he could stop Greg concocting another ludicrous story, but interrupting him would only make things worse.

"Scandivaria?" said Mrs Spinetti. "Where is that exactly?"

"It's one of those Norwegian countries, you know," said Greg.

Lewis was horrified to see Susie nodding. "That's right, Mum."

"So, anyway, this Larry character steals these treasures and hides them in St Andrews," Greg continued relentlessly.

"You mean like the hammer Sven found in our garage?" said Dad.

"Correct!" said Greg, stabbing a finger in the air. "You see Sven is one of the SAPS."

"Saps?" said Mr Spinetti.

"The Scandivarian Antiquities Protection Squad. He's been sent to get the treasures back. Haven't you, Sven?"

Thor was busy shovelling spaghetti into his mouth but he nodded in confirmation.

"I don't quite see what any of this has to do with Garth," said Mum.

"I'm, uh, hanging out with Sven as research for my next film, *Treasures of the Hidden Kingdom*," said Makepeace, flashing a charming smile. "Now, we're strangers in this area, so the kids were helping us find our way around."

"Isn't it a bit dangerous, chasing after international criminals?" asked Mr Spinetti with a frown.

Makepeace laughed. "That Larry is a cream puff," he said. "He couldn't hurt a fly if it was tied up and blindfolded."

"So what happened to Sven?" asked Mrs Spinetti. "He looks like a bus fell on him."

"I slipped on the ice," said Thor, pouring himself another glass of home brew. He pushed away his empty plate and smacked his lips. "Is there any dessert?"

There was trifle, with cream and custard. Lots of it. By the time they were done, Lewis was so stuffed he could hardly move. Loki and his evil plans seemed a million miles away from this feast.

Once the table was cleared, even Susie looked exhausted.

"We've put out camp beds and sleeping bags, so everybody should have a good night's sleep," said Mrs Spinetti.

"Don't worry about that," Greg yawned. "I feel like I could sleep for a week."

The brothers had been set up in the music room. They unpacked the bags they had brought from home earlier and got into their pyjamas.

"It doesn't feel right, going to sleep while Loki's out there with the Yggdrasil Seed," said Lewis, zipping himself into his sleeping bag.

"Relax," yawned Greg, thumping his head down on his pillow. "Nothing's going to grow in this weather, not even a magic tree."

"I suppose you're right," said Lewis. And in spite of his worrying, he was asleep as soon as he closed his eyes.

He awoke with a start to find Susie was shaking them both out of their sleep.

"Wake up, you guys! Come and see what's happened!"

"Now what?" moaned Greg, rubbing his eyes.

"It's springtime!" Susie announced. "The sun's out and the snow's melting."

Lewis tried to leap out of bed but got tangled in his sleeping bag and rolled on to the floor with a thud. When he made it to the window he saw it was true. There was a brilliant summer sun in the sky and there were only a few traces of snow left on the hedges and trees.

"The trouble is," said Greg, "this could be bad news."

"Right," Lewis agreed. "If Loki's switched off the winter, he must have a good reason."

"You don't suppose he's flown back to his own planet, do you?" Susie suggested hopefully.

"Don't you remember, Sven told us he wants to get back to Asgard," said Lewis, "the home of the gods."

"Oh, yes, like that's not an alien planet or anything," Susie retorted with heavy sarcasm.

"Let's go talk to Sven," Greg suggested.

Thor was bedded down in the room that used to belong to Susie's older brother Frankie. He was propped up on his pillows flicking through one of the film magazines Frankie had left behind. "There's a lot of pictures of that Makepeace in here," he grunted. "You would think he was a big shot."

"Sven, the snow's all melted," Susie reported.

"Loki must be up to something," said Greg.

Thor laid the magazine aside and grimaced. "He will be planting the seed to grow the new Yggdrasil."

"Where?" asked Lewis.

Thor pondered for a few moments then said, "It will be on high ground, most likely a place of mystic power."

"Mystic power?" echoed Greg. "That's not something they put on a map."

"How about Hallowhill?" Susie offered.

"That's a good bet," Lewis agreed. "The name Hallow means holy and there are Pictish graves up there."

"That sounds pretty mystical to me," said Greg. "How about it, Sven?"

Thor nodded grimly. "You should check it out."

"You can see it from my bedroom window," said Susie. "Come on!"

The boys followed her upstairs. The walls of her room were covered in posters of football and hockey players and the shelves behind her bed were packed with sporting trophies.

The three of them crowded round the window and stared over the rooftops towards Hallowhill. "Oh, isn't that just great!" Greg exclaimed.

Hallowhill was swathed in a thick cloud of mist that rose like a huge smoky column high up into the clouds.

"I suppose that could be water vapour from the melting snow," said Susie.

"It might be," Greg agreed, "but I'll bet you anything that Loki's wrapped a mist around Hallowhill to hide what he's up to."

When they reported back to Thor, he agreed with their conclusion. "He is hiding the Yggdrasil from view while it grows."

He tried to climb out of bed but his leg gave out under him and Greg and Lewis had to catch him. "It's no good," he groaned as the boys helped him settle back against his pillows. "You'll have to go without me. But you must catch up with Loki and stop him."

"Should we tell Mum and Dad?" asked Lewis.

"By the time we explain it all to them, Loki will be long gone," said Greg. "No, it's us or nobody."

"What about Garth?" said Lewis. "Maybe he'll want in on this."

"I looked in on him," said Susie. "He's completely zonked out."

"Too much of the home brew," said Thor. "Best leave him to sleep it off."

"We could still do with some help," said Lewis anxiously.

"You have the two treasures," Thor reminded him, "the Ring Draupnir and the Shoes of Vidar. Use them wisely and the victory will be yours."

"It's all right for them," Susie complained. "What about me? I don't have a treasure."

"You shall have the greatest treasure of all," said Thor. He leaned down to pick Mjolnir from the floor and offered it to her. "To replace the hockey stick you lost."

Susie took the hammer and swung it from side to side in her hand.

"How is she doing that?" Greg exclaimed. "I couldn't even lift it."

"Mjolnir can only be wielded by me," Thor explained, "or a person I entrust it to."

Susie tossed the hammer into the air and caught it as easily as she would catch a tennis ball.

"Now, Susie, you are a warrior maid of Asgard," Thor told her.

Susie grinned. "Cool!"

"We can't waste a second," Greg reminded them. "Let's go!"

They dressed quickly and set out on the path leading to Hallowhill. Greg moved along briskly; the Shoes of Vidar made it hard not to break into a run. Susie had Mjolnir tucked into the straps of her backpack. Lewis fingered the ring in his pocket. It didn't feel like much protection against whatever Loki was likely to throw at them.

When they arrived at the foot of the hill, the quiet flow of the Kinnessburn below them had been transformed into a rushing torrent by the melted snow. The trees that dotted the lower levels of the slope were still flecked with white. Above and beyond them the great bank of mist completely enveloped the summit. They climbed up to the edge of the misty wall and stared up. It seemed to go on and on forever, right up to the sky.

Greg drew a deep breath. "Okay, this is it. We don't want anybody getting lost in there, so stick together."

"Give me your hands and hold tight," said Susie. "That way we can't get separated."

Hands joined, they plunged into the mist and were swallowed up in a shroud of darkness.

13. TURN LEFT AT NIFLHEIM

Susie's fingers were interlocked tightly with the boys' as the three of them walked through the murk, their boots crunching on the frosty grass. The higher they climbed, the thinner the mist grew, until they could glimpse something of immense bulk looming ahead. Eyes fixed on the dark shape, they pressed on until the mist cleared to reveal an amazing sight.

"Wow!" said Lewis.

"Wow is right," Greg agreed.

Susie gazed upwards, her eyes wide with wonder. "It's an impressive piece of bioengineering, that's for sure," she said.

The newly created Yggdrasil had roots like bridge cables that had burrowed deep down into the hill. The trunk of the great tree was thirty metres across. It rose up like a skyscraper, soaring higher and higher to vanish among the clouds.

"That is the biggest tree I have ever seen," said Greg.

"I expect it's the biggest tree anyone's ever seen," said Lewis.

"Up until now I always thought Jack and the Beanstalk was just a story," said Susie in an awestruck voice.

"It's going to be a tough climb," said Greg.

"Maybe not," said Lewis. "Take a closer look."

Following his pointing finger, the other two saw that there was a narrow ledge jutting out from the trunk. It went right around the tree, passing between the branches and winding upwards, like a spiral stairway leading up to the sky. "It's like a track running up to the top," said Lewis.

"Well, that makes things a lot easier," said Greg with a grin.

"And to think I brought rope and everything," said Susie, plucking at the straps of her backpack. She sounded a little disappointed.

"It makes sense," said Lewis. "If the Yggdrasil is supposed to link the Nine Realms of the Universe, like Thor said, there would have to be a path you could follow."

"Come on then," said Greg. "We don't have any time to waste if we're going to catch up with Loki."

He hurried to the base of the tree and started up the spiral path. They went up in single file with Susie following Greg and Lewis bringing up the rear. After a while Greg stopped to catch his breath. "Is everybody okay?" he asked.

Lewis took the chance to look down and wished he hadn't. The summit of Hallowhill was a green blur far below. Overhead, he could see stars blinking through the mist.

"We're fine, Greg. Stop slacking," said Susie.

Greg grunted at her and resumed the climb. When they at last drew clear of the mist they were surrounded by brilliant starlight and the immense tree stretched endlessly away into the void above them.

"This is completely impossible," said Lewis. "It looks like we're climbing up into outer space."

"We're in some kind of dimensional rift," Susie told him. "Don't worry about it."

"Don't worry?!" Lewis exclaimed. Susie paid no attention, so he decided to save his breath for the climb.

All around them leafy branches stretched out across the starry sky. The leaves were bright green, veined with silver. When Lewis laid a hand against the bark it felt smooth and soft, just what you'd expect, he supposed, from a tree that was newly born that morning.

An excited cry from Greg made him look up. His brother had arrived at a great branch that extended directly outward from the spiral path they had been following. When Lewis and Susie caught up with him, they saw that it was completely level and flattened on the top, so that it would be easy to walk along it.

"This must be the way to Asgard," Greg declared.

"How can you be sure of that?" Lewis asked dubiously.

"Well, there isn't a signpost, if that's what you want, but it's the first route off the tree."

"There's a mist out there, kind of like the one we came through down below," said Susie. "Maybe Loki's using it to cover his tracks again."

"We don't have time to mess about," said Greg. "Let's go!"

He set out boldly along the wooden path. Susie and Lewis fell into step behind him and they marched towards the cloud bank. When the first wisps of mist touched Lewis' face, he felt the hairs on his neck bristle and had a powerful impulse to turn back.

"Maybe this isn't the right way," he said.

"Will you stop complaining?" Greg snapped. "We'll know soon enough."

They entered the cloud and it swirled about them, chilly and dank. Unlike the mist surrounding the foot of the Yggdrasil, it clung to them as if it was trying to seep through their skin into their bones. Lewis kept his eyes on his feet, nervous of stepping off the path.

Susie said abruptly, "Hey, we're not on wood any more."

Greg stamped his feet. "You're right," he said. "It's solid ground."

They carried on and the mist gradually thinned to allow them glimpses of an unearthly landscape. Narrow spires of pale rock stretched up like skeletal fingers while the ground on all sides was covered in heaps of dry, white ash. Tendrils of mist twisted and coiled about them, clutching them in a chill embrace.

As they pressed forward, they bunched together protectively. Straining his eyes in the gloom, Lewis was sure he could make out shadowy figures drifting by silently at the extreme edge of his vision. "There's something moving out there," he said softly. Something about the place made him want to whisper.

"And do you hear that noise?" said Susie.

"It's just the wind," said Greg, though he didn't sound confident.

"There isn't any wind," Susie pointed out.

"It sounds like... voices," said Lewis.

But they weren't like any voices he had ever heard before. They were shrill, keening a high-pitched, eerie song filled with sadness and dread.

"This doesn't feel much like Asgard," said Greg, "not unless the gods have an extremely creepy decorating style."

Suddenly Susie squealed. The shock made Lewis jump. He wasn't used to her being frightened.

Greg grabbed her by the shoulder. "What happened? Are you all right?"

Susie trembled. "Something touched me. It felt like fingers... fingers made of ice."

Lewis spotted one of the shadow forms drifting by then disappearing into the mist.

"What was that?" Susie breathed.

Greg shot Lewis a demanding look. "Come on, Lewis, you're the expert. Where are we?"

"I'll find out," said Lewis. He slipped the ring onto his finger and immediately felt a buzzing in his head. It took a moment for his thoughts to clear then he said, "Oh, no!"

"What is it?" Susie asked anxiously.

"We're in Niflheim," said Lewis, "the Kingdom of Ghosts."

Greg swallowed hard. "Lewis, have you any idea how completely bad that sounds?"

"We'd better get out of here," said Susie, backing up.

They had the sense that a multitude of restless spirits were closing in on them, hidden from view by the mist. The fearful, dreary song was growing louder.

"Did anybody bring a compass?" Greg asked. "Because I've got all turned around."

"This mist, it confuses everything," said Susie.

"Follow me," said Lewis.

The ring was tugging him in the right direction, but as soon as he took a step, a spectral shape flickered across his path and a breath of chilling vapour struck him in the face. He pulled back with a shiver and bumped into Greg.

"Steady, Lewis," said his brother encouragingly. "I'm pretty sure ghosts can't hurt you. Pretty sure."

"They're not even real," said Susie, though her voice was quavering.

"This place seems real enough to me," Lewis muttered, moving forward.

Every few steps an eerie apparition flitted across his sight and cold fear clutched at his heart, but he pressed on with the others right at his back. Finally the mist parted and they could see the way ahead.

"There's the path!" Lewis exclaimed.

Before them lay the great flattened branch that led out of Niflheim.

"Well, don't hang about. Let's go!" urged Greg, pushing Susie and Lewis on ahead of him.

They hurried down the wooden path to the welcome safety of the Yggdrasil. Leaning against the trunk to catch his breath, Lewis removed the ring. It was a relief to have the buzzing in his head subside.

"Are you okay, Spinny?" Greg asked. "You looked a bit shaken up back there."

"I'm fine now," said Susie. "Aliens and monsters are one thing, but that place – uuurgh!" She shuddered as she glanced back in the direction of Niflheim.

"You'd better keep that ring handy, Lewis," said Greg. "One more wrong turn like that could be the end of us."

Once again he led the way up. As they climbed, Lewis felt something dropping onto his hair. He brushed it off and saw that there were flakes of dry wood stuck to his fingers.

"Look at the tree," he said. "The bark's drying out and crumbling."

"Right, and have you noticed the path crunching under your feet?" asked Susie. "It didn't do that when we started out."

They gazed around them and saw that the leaves, once bright green, now looked bent and tired, their colour fading against the background of stars.

"It's because Loki used up all the life in the seed in order to make it grow so fast," Lewis guessed. "It's ageing and dying just as quickly."

"You mess with nature and that's what you get," said Greg ruefully.

"We'd better make tracks," said Susie, "before it falls apart."

There came a crack from above and they looked up to see one of the smaller branches snapping off the tree. They flattened themselves against the trunk as the loose branch came spinning past them, end over end. It hit another branch below, jarring that loose too.

"Right, let's go," Greg urged. "And keep your eyes peeled for a way off this thing."

As they hurried, the wood underfoot cracked and crunched. It was like walking across a floor covered in breakfast cereal. At last they came to another path that branched off and stretched away into a black cloud.

"What do you think, Lewis?" Greg asked.

Lewis slipped the ring on and placed one foot on the outstretched branch. He shook his head. "This leads to Muspell, the Realm of Fire."

"Oh great!" Greg groaned. "There must be some way to get to Asgard."

"It will be higher up," said Susie. "Just keep going."

Upward they went, with showers of dead leaves raining down on them from above. Deep cracks appeared in the trunk and more branches were snapping off every few seconds.

"There, that's got to be it!" Greg exclaimed, pointing to another path jutting out from the trunk.

Lewis put on the ring and tried it. "No good," he

sighed. "This is the way to Jotunheim, the Land of the Giants."

"If we don't find another way off soon," said Greg, "we might have to take our chances there. Otherwise we'll be in for a long drop."

Susie forced a brave smile. "And nobody thought to pack parachutes?" She gave Greg a prod. "On you go then."

Flakes of bark and dead leaves were falling on them steadily now and their feet were sinking into the path like it was sand. They struggled on, trying to ignore the creaking and groaning of the dying Yggdrasil.

"There, check that out, Lewis!" Greg ordered urgently, pointing at another path up ahead. It ran out across the empty sky and vanished into a white cloud.

Lewis slipped on the ring and placed a foot on the branch.

"Yes, that's Asgard out there!" he exclaimed.

"Are you sure?" Greg asked.

"Yes, yes!" Lewis insisted, flashing the ring at him.

"Just in time," said Greg.

He strode out along the limb, but at his first step the wood cracked and splinters rained down into the void below.

"No, Greg!" Susie exclaimed. She grabbed his arm and dragged him back. "It's too far gone to hold our weight."

"Well, we can't just stay here," said Lewis. "The whole tree is going to fall apart any minute now."

"Hang on a second," said Greg. He pulled the Shoes of Vidar from his backpack and swapped them for his boots. "With these I can practically walk on air."

"And what about us?" asked Susie.

"You said you'd brought rope," said Greg. "Get it out."

Susie handed him the rope. Greg quickly tied one end around his waist and gave her the other. "You two hang on to that," he said. "I'm making a run for Asgard."

He raced off down the long wooden path, the rope uncoiling behind him. The branch cracked and sagged as he ran but the magical shoes kept him from losing his footing. Susie and Lewis wound their end of the rope tightly around their hands and watched as Greg disappeared into the cloud.

All at once the rope went taut.

"There's no choice now," said Susie. "We have to go for it."

"Let's run," Lewis agreed.

Clutching the rope, Susie raced along the branch with Lewis right behind her. They made it a few metres before the wood broke apart beneath them and they plunged downward through the empty air.

"Hang on, Lewis!" Susie cried.

Lewis twisted the rope around his hands so tightly it

burned his skin and his fingers turned white. Dangling over the void, he glanced back to where the Yggdrasil was in its final throes. It reminded him of a film he once saw of a skyscraper being demolished. With a dull boom, the gigantic tree burst apart in a shower of dead leaves and shattered bark that scattered across the starry void.

14. THE ROUGH GUIDE TO ASGARD

Tearing his eyes away from the horrifying emptiness below, Lewis looked up to where Susie was clinging fiercely to their lifeline. Grunting at the exertion, she was hauling herself upward inch by inch.

Lewis tried to do the same. As he shifted his hands the rope burned his fingers and his muscles ached as though streams of fire were running through them. He was shocked by a sudden jolt on the rope.

"Greg's pulling us up, Lewis!" Susie shouted down at him. "Just hang on a bit longer."

Lewis peered past her to the white cloud that spread right across their vision. With each jerk of the rope it came closer, until they were engulfed by it and he could see nothing at all. The strain on his arms was almost unbearable, but he clung on grimly and felt himself ascending.

Above him came a triumphant whoop. Emerging from the murk, he saw an outcrop of rock, like the edge of a cliff, jutting out into the emptiness. Susie and Greg were perched together on the edge. Between them, they hauled Lewis up the rest of the way.

Once they had dragged him up beside them, the three of them retreated from the edge and collapsed side by side on a stretch of grass, panting for breath.

"I didn't think we were going to make it," Lewis gasped.

"I couldn't have pulled you both up if the magic shoes hadn't kept me rooted to the ground," said Greg.

Susie lifted her head off the grass. "I've always said it's important to have the right footwear."

When at last they had recovered their breath, they got to their feet and took a proper look at the landscape before them.

"This is it," said Lewis, "Asgard, the home of the gods, the Golden Realm."

Greg gazed about him, unimpressed. "Frankly, it's a bit of a dump."

Lewis had to agree. He had expected Asgard to be a riot of colour, bright with sunlight and vibrant with life, a home worthy of the Viking gods.

It wasn't.

The sky overhead was a sullen grey, clogged with gloomy clouds. The tall trees drooped like weary old men, their dull leaves like wrinkled hands. The drab hillsides were mottled with banks of withered flowers, their petals shrivelled and dry. In the distance was a city surrounded by a wall, but even from a distance it looked ancient and abandoned. The worst thing was the silence. There was no birdsong – not even the whisper of a breeze.

"It is a bit of a let down," Lewis agreed.

"Well, it's obvious what's happened," said Susie, rolling up the rope and stuffing it back in her pack.

"Not to me it isn't," said Greg.

"Look, if you wander off and leave your computer," Susie explained, "it shuts itself down to save power. The same thing has happened here. Asgard's been uninhabited for centuries, so it's shut itself down."

"But if Loki reaches Odin's throne, he can boot it up again," said Lewis.

"Right," said Susie. "And once it's back online, who knows what he'll do with all that power."

"That's what we're here to stop," said Greg. "Come on."

They crossed over an arched bridge, its stonework pitted and stained with dead moss. The stream below was still and scummy. There was no sign of life in the motionless waters.

A wide roadway paved with cracked grey flagstones led to the city. As the three youngsters advanced, their footsteps rang hollow in the still air. In front of them the wall rose up like a cliff made of huge granite blocks.

The arched gateway was decorated with carvings that were so blurred, it was impossible to make out what they were supposed to be. The wooden gates hung tiredly on their rusted hinges, leaving a gap for the visitors to pass through.

The city beyond must once have been a wonderful sight. Buildings of every shape and material rose in tier upon tier against the sky, but over them all hung an air of long abandonment, as though they had lain empty and derelict for centuries.

As they walked down the broad avenue between the huge buildings, Greg said, "This is a big place, Lewis. You'd better get that brainy ring out so we can find our way around."

"I suppose so," Lewis agreed reluctantly.

He slipped the ring on to his finger and at once the familiar buzzing filled his head. Although it was feeding him lots of information, it made it hard to concentrate, like having one of Greg's favourite metal bands dinning in his ears.

He pointed back the way they had come and said, "The wall of Asgard was built by a giant stonemason with the aid of his stallion Svadilfari, but he was cheated out of his payment by Loki."

"No surprise there, then," said Greg. "What's that building up there on the crag, the one with the horns?"

Lewis shifted his gaze to the square stone building that stood alone on a table of rock. From the flat roof a pair of pillars extended into the sky, bending inward towards each other and tapering to points as they rose.

"It looks kind of like the observatory on Balgay Hill in Dundee," said Susie. "Except for the horns, of course."

"That's the Himinbjorg," Lewis informed them, "the Gatehouse of Heimdall, guardian of the Bifrost." He turned and pointed to another building constructed in the shape of a great ship with a dragon prow. "That's the home of the god Njord, the god of the sea."

Further on he gestured towards a stone-built fortress where an anvil sat outside the gate. "That's Bilskirnir, the home of Thor," he said. "There are 540 rooms inside and 300 suits of armour." Unable to stop the words tumbling from his lips, he added, "Down that way is Sessrumir, the hall of Freya. She's the goddess of love and beauty."

"All right, Lewis, that's enough," Greg interrupted.

"Greg's right," said Susie. "It is starting to get annoying."

"Don't tell us anything else unless we really need to know it," said Greg.

Lewis rubbed his head. "Okay, but I was going to point out Ydalir, the hall of Ull."

"Don't bother!" Greg told him. "Just get us to Odin's palace."

Biting his lip, Lewis pointed down a wide street on their left.

"Thanks," said Greg. "Let's go."

As they pressed on, Lewis had to bite his lip to keep from telling them about every spot they passed. Keeping it all bottled up inside made his head ache more than ever, and it was a huge relief when a great marble palace came into view, with brass doors and a pair of stone ravens peering down from the roof.

"That's Odin's palace right there," he said, yanking off the ring. At once the buzzing in his head stopped, but the ache was still there.

They halted in their tracks, for bent over the lock of the brass door was a familiar figure in a long dark coat. Loki was probing the mechanism with a needle, and when he heard a click, he stepped back with a sigh of satisfaction. The door swung open, revealing a shadowy hallway within.

"Not so fast, Larry!" Greg called out. "That's breaking and entering."

Loki swung round and anger flashed in his dark green eyes.

"You! What do I have to do to get rid of you? Use bug spray?"

Susie reached behind her and pulled out Mjolnir. "Careful, Greg," she warned. "Those shoes won't protect you if he's got a ray gun or something."

Undaunted, Greg stepped forward boldly. Loki flung up a warning hand and sparks danced between his fingers. Frowning in concentration, he struggled to summon a bolt of fire, but nothing came. He finally lowered his arm with a snarl of frustration.

"It looks like your powers are dead, just like everything else in this place," said Greg, advancing towards him with Susie and Lewis at his side.

"Don't be too sure of that," Loki sneered. "You should know by now I always have a few tricks up my sleeve."

Shoving a hand inside his coat, he pulled out a metal disk the size of a frisbee. It was marked with runes all round the edge and there was a blue jewel in the centre.

"This is another little trinket I picked up in St Andrews," Loki informed them with a thin smile. "The Shield Svalin."

"That's one of the treasures Thor told us about," Lewis recalled.

"It doesn't look like much," said Greg with a shrug.

Loki thrust the shield out in front of him and immediately all three of them felt some invisible force hurl them back. They stumbled backwards until the pressure stopped and they saw that the air before them was shimmering, as though filled with raindrops.

Greg stretched out a hand and gave a grunt as it bumped against something solid. "He's put up some kind of a wall," he said beating at it with his fist.

"It's a force field," said Susie. "Let me have a go."

She took a swing with Mjolnir, but her blow rebounded off the unseen barrier.

"I don't think you're man enough to handle that hammer, toots," Loki taunted her.

"I told you not to call me toots!" Susie yelled.

In a fury she swung Mjolnir again and struck the barrier an even fiercer blow that made it boom like a giant bell. The impact reverberated right through to the other side and sent Loki stumbling backwards. Visibly shaken, he straightened his hat and leaned the shield against the marble wall.

"I'd love to stay and watch you beating your brains in against this thing," he said, "but I've got business inside." He jerked a thumb at the palace, then turned on his heel and disappeared through the doorway.

Susie rained blow after blow down on the barrier until she was red-faced and panting. Lewis clapped his hands over his ears, which were ringing with the noise.

Greg caught her by the arm. "Spinny, you'd better stop that before you hurt yourself," he said.

"Well, what are we supposed to do then?" Susie demanded breathlessly. "Just stand around while that creep takes over the universe?"

Greg pressed the flat of his hand against the barrier. "Maybe we can find a way around it."

"I'll bet he's blocked off the whole palace," said Lewis.

"Fine!" Greg snapped. "Why don't you put the ring on and see if it can tell you what to do?"

"It doesn't work like that," Lewis mumbled. He put a hand in his pocket and squeezed the ring between his fingers. It was then that the answer came to him.

"Susie," he said excitedly, "do you remember how Thor used the hammer to snatch the ring off Loki?"

"Sure," said Susie. "It's magnetic."

"Do you think you could do the same thing with that shield?"

Greg shot him an approving grin. "Lewis, I think you're on to something!"

"I don't know how he made it work," said Susie, "but I'll give it a try."

Gripping Mjolnir in both hands, she pointed the hammer at the shield and concentrated. "Come on," she muttered. "Come to Susie, you wee dustbin lid."

At first nothing happened, then Lewis noticed that the shield was quivering. "Keep it up," he urged. "It's starting to work."

Susie gritted her teeth and focused on drawing the shield towards her. It slid forward on its edge away from the wall, then rose into the air. All at once it started spinning and flew towards them. Greg took a step back and Lewis instinctively threw up an arm to protect himself, but Susie didn't budge an inch.

With a clang, the shield crashed into the force barrier. There was a terrible screeching sound and sparks flew everywhere, then the shield clattered to the ground. The metal was scorched and the jewel in the centre had burnt to a cinder.

The shimmer in the air had vanished. Lewis walked forwards with his arm extended. "The force wall is down," he announced.

"It short-circuited itself!" Susie exclaimed in delight. "Good thinking, Lewis!"

Greg stooped to pick up the shield. "Ouch!" he complained, sucking his finger. "It's blazing hot!"

"It won't work now anyway," said Lewis. "Like Susie said, it's burnt out."

"Well, what are we waiting for?" said Susie, brandishing the hammer. "Let's go and catch that rat!"

They hurried inside the palace then skidded to a halt. In the middle of the entrance hall loomed a ferocious looking dragon, its head almost brushing the rafters. Its gaping jaws showed a double row of fangs as sharp as daggers and its upraised claws looked like they could tear a tank in half.

Greg reeled back and grabbed his brother's arm. "You could have warned us about this, Lewis!"

Susie hefted Mjolnir to strike, then relaxed with a laugh. "It's okay, guys. It's just a statue."

"Sure, I knew that," said Greg, recovering his swagger. Even though he could see now that the dragon was made of stone, he still kept a wary eye on it.

"We still have a bit of a problem though," said Susie. "There's a dozen different ways we could go from here."

Beyond the dragon countless passages and stairways opened up before them.

"Lewis, we'll never find our way without help," said Greg.

"All right," said Lewis, "but don't complain if I give you a guided tour."

He slipped the ring on and its power hit him with a jolt. The layout of the palace was so complex, its history so ancient, that there was more information than he could sort through. It was like a toy train set inside his head, with a hundred trains zooming around it all at once, in constant danger of collision.

Rubbing his brow, he waved his hand vaguely. "This way... I think."

"You think?" said Greg. "You're supposed to know."

"Take it easy, Greg," said Susie. "Can you not see it's stressing him out?"

"Okay, Lewis," said Greg, his tone softening, "you go on ahead and we'll follow."

Lewis led them up a stairway and through an arch. They passed down a long corridor lined with statues of once heroic figures who now stood with sagging shoulders, their faces weary and depressed. They walked through halls where tables were laid out for feasts – but the plates and goblets were empty and covered in layers of dust.

On the walls were tapestries, their colours long faded with age, depicting tired deer slouching among dead, leafless trees. Mud coloured carpets were rough and threadbare beneath their feet. All through the palace there was the dismal air of neglect.

When Lewis tried to tell the others about the areas they were passing through, for the ring compelled him to try, he found it impossible to make sense. "Sheep, margarine, loophole," he muttered. "I mean extra frog cappuccino... Och, the words keep jumbling up."

"Give it up, Lewis," said Greg. "Just keep walking."

At last they came to a set of double doors on which was carved what had once been a battle scene, but now all the warriors had slumped to the ground, too weak to lift their weapons. The doors were ajar, allowing the three youngsters to pass through into a hall as long as a football pitch. The walls on both sides were lined with suits of dull, empty armour topped by helmets decorated with drooping horns and moulded wings.

At the far end was a raised dais supporting a throne. Approaching it with a jaunty step was Loki. He hopped on to the dais, spun round and plumped himself down on the throne.

"Hel-lo, Asgard!" he exclaimed in a happy sing-song voice.

Instantly, a shimmering glow enveloped the dais. A deep throbbing note rang out, like a chord being struck on an enormous piano. It echoed all around them, like an unseen orchestra tuning up

"That's right, I'm back, baby!" Loki declared, his green eyes flashing with wicked delight.

15. RAGNAROK AND A HARD PLACE

Lewis yanked off the ring, ridding himself of the jangling in his head.

Susie grasped his arm to steady him and guided him along behind Greg, who was striding forward to challenge the god of mischief.

At the sight of them, a hateful sneer curled Loki's lip.

"You three have more luck than is decent. I could have sworn the shield would stop you cold."

"Take it from a top goal scorer," said Susie, "there's no such thing as a perfect defence."

"You know," said Loki, "I've just about had it with you kids and your meddling."

"You're wasting your time," Greg told him. "This place is as dead as a doughnut. Why don't you come back to Earth so you and Thor can talk it over?"

Loki laughed contemptuously. "Earth? That dung heap! It will be a hot day in Niflheim before you see me there again. In fact, it may be time to do away with it once and for all."

"I don't think so, Larry," said Greg. "We're here to cancel Rubberduck."

Loki slammed an angry fist down on the arm of his throne. "That's Ragnarok, you bonehead! *Ragnarok!*"

Greg shrugged. "I've heard it both ways."

"You're pretty full of yourself, aren't you?" said Susie. "You think you can just waltz in and take over the universe."

"Pretty much," Loki agreed.

The rows of torches lining the walls suddenly sprouted flame and the lanterns hanging from the vaulted ceiling blossomed with light. There was a resounding CLANK as the rows of armour drew themselves up to attention, gripping axes, spears and swords in their iron gauntlets. All of a sudden they flashed in the firelight, as though polished up for inspection.

"Asgard is powering up," said Loki slyly, "and I'm the only god in town."

Susie leaned in close to Greg and asked. "What do we do now?"

"He's not so tough," said Greg. "Between the three of us we can drag him off that throne before he can do any damage. Ready, Lewis?"

Lewis nodded numbly. He was so shaky from the effects of the ring, he couldn't think of anything to do except follow Greg's lead.

Greg started forward. In response Loki snapped his fingers and a ring of fire sprang up all round the dais. The three youngsters drew back reflexively as a wave of heat washed over them.

"Like I was saying," sneered Loki, "I'm the boss here now, and there's nobody to help you."

From behind them came a series of clangs and clashes. Lewis looked round and saw that one by one the suits of armour were pulling away from the walls and lurching toward them.

"Boys," said Susie through gritted teeth, "I hate to say this, but it looks like we've got a battle on our hands."

Loki looked on smugly as the empty suits of armour closed in on the three mortals. Their movements were slow but relentless, and their raised weapons glittered dangerously.

"You can't stop us with a lot of scrap metal," Greg challenged him.

"I'll say this for you, kid," said Loki, "you've got more nerve than a rotten tooth."

The three youngsters drew together as the suits of armour clanked closer and closer.

"We should rush him," said Susie, "before he gets even more powerful."

"What, through a wall of fire?" Lewis exclaimed.

"Maybe if you put the ring on, it will tell you how to switch the flames off," Greg suggested.

Lewis groaned at the thought of the headache he was in for, but it was worth a try. He pulled the ring out of his pocket, but before he could slide it on to his finger, the nearest metal warrior took a swing at him with a two-handed sword.

Greg snatched him out of the way, but as the blade flashed past his nose, Lewis dropped the ring and saw it roll off between a pair of iron feet.

"Rats!" Greg exclaimed. He started to go after the ring, but Susie hooked his arm to keep him back.

"Don't be stupid!" she said. "One of those things will have your head off!"

More armoured suits were pressing forward.

"We'd better get out of here while we still can," said Lewis.

"Right!" Greg agreed.

Moving nimbly, thanks to the Shoes of Vidar, he charged through the remaining gap, bumping two metal guards aside. Lewis and Susie darted after him, but they could see that suits of armour had come to life all over the hall. They had completely blocked off their route to the door.

"We'll never make it that way," said Greg. "Quick, up those stairs!"

He pointed to a stairway in a corner of the room. They made a dash for it, but as they reached the first step, a suit of armour wielding a club lurched out of the shadows to block their path.

"Leave this to me," said Susie, her eyes blazing.

She took a swing with Mjolnir and sent the helmet flying off the armoured shoulders with a loud clang. The headless warrior staggered for a moment, then fell over. Susie jumped over the heap of metal with a whoop and the three of them raced up the stairs.

The metal warriors tried to follow, but as they crowded on to the narrow stair, they got tangled up with each other and went clattering back down to the bottom.

"Those boys have got a lot to learn about teamwork," Susie commented with a grin.

They ducked under an arch and down a passage that took them to a long gallery. Lined up along one wall of the gallery were a dozen dwarfs in pointed helmets, each clutching a double-headed axe.

"Whoa! More trouble!" Greg exclaimed, pulling the other two back.

Lewis squinted at the dwarfs and breathed a sigh of relief. "It's okay. They're just statues, like the dragon was."

Susie eyed the dwarfs as they hurried past them to

the other end of the gallery. "They may not be very big," she noted, "but they look pretty fierce."

They passed through a doorway at the far end and came to a corridor that branched off in two directions.

"We need to find a way around the throne room that will take us back to the entrance," said Greg. "So how about it, Lewis? Which way do we go?"

Lewis rubbed his brow, trying to remember the layout of the palace the way it had appeared to him while he was wearing the ring, but his recollection of the halls, chambers and corridors was all scrambled, like a deck of cards tossed into the air.

"It's hard to sort it all out," he groaned. His head started to throb like it did when he was wearing the ring. "That door there," he said, pointing.

"Are you sure?" asked Greg.

Lewis shook his head. "It's more a hunch than anything else."

"Well, it's all we've got," said Susie. "Let's go!"

They entered a new gallery lined with tapestries of forest scenes that fluttered as they passed, as if disturbed by a gust of wind. Lewis was sure he glimpsed beastly eyes lurking among the woven trees, spying on them as they hurried by.

"What's that growling?" said Greg. "It sounds like it's coming from those pictures."

"Best if we don't find out," said Lewis, pushing him on.

The next door led to another gallery. The walls here were hung on both sides with long mirrors made from polished metal. As they passed between them, hundreds of reflections sprang up, like an army leaping out of ambush.

Lewis paused to peer at himself in the shiny metal. To his astonishment, his reflection pointed an accusing finger at him and yelled, "Where do you think you're going?"

"Shut up, Lewis!" Greg hissed.

Before Lewis could open his mouth to protest, all of Greg's reflections leaned towards him. "*Shut up, Lewis!*" they shouted in chorus.

All of Lewis' reflections now jumped up and down, yelling, "Here they are! They're in the mirror gallery!"

Images of Susie all down the gallery cupped their hands around their mouths and shouted, "Guards! Guards! Come and nab them before they get away!"

"Talk about being your own worst enemy," said Susie.

Covering their ears to block out the din, they barged through the door and banged it shut behind them. Back in the gallery, their reflections were still raising the alarm.

"As long as we're in the palace, Loki will find us," said Greg. "The throne lets him control everything in the place."

"Right," Susie agreed. "We need to find a way out before he brings the roof down on us or something."

They were now in a large banqueting hall where wooden benches ran down both sides of a long table. The walls were decorated with hunting trophies, drooping antlers and sad-looking animal skulls.

"We should keep going this way," said Lewis, pointing to the door at the far end.

They had no sooner reached it than there came a grating, clomping sound from the other side. Freezing in fright, they watched in horror as something enormous took a huge bite out of the door. Through the hole they saw the snout of a huge lizard chewing on the wood.

"Oh no," groaned Lewis. "More bad news!"

"It's that stone dragon we saw at the entrance," said Greg. "Loki's brought it to life and sent it after us."

"Oh he's a right stinker!" Susie exclaimed bitterly.

"We need to go back the other way," said Greg, leading the retreat. "At least the mirrors won't eat us."

The dragon took another bite out of the door, which was all the encouragement they needed to take to their heels. However, even as they fled, the door to the mirror gallery was smashed open and a troop of stone dwarfs came marching out, brandishing their axes.

"Those guys!" Greg groaned. "We're right in the mincer now!"

"Look!" Susie cried. "There's a wee door there, under those antlers!" They bolted for that door as the dragon burst into the hall and the dwarfs formed a column and marched after them.

"In here!" snapped Susie, flinging open the door and bundling the brothers through. They stumbled into a room furnished with a table and a few chairs. There was a window in the far wall.

"That was a bit of a gamble, Spinny," Greg grumbled. "For all you knew, this could have been a broom cupboard."

"And there's no way out," Lewis noted glumly.

"Oh shut up and help me block the door," Susie ordered.

They piled the few items of furniture against the door. From outside they could hear the stone dragon's rasping breath.

"That won't hold for long," said Lewis gazing at the flimsy barricade.

Susie dashed to the window and when she turned round she was grinning. "It's okay, there's a ledge out here."

The boys joined her at the window and when Lewis looked out his stomach lurched. "It's only a couple of feet wide and we're three floors up!" he gasped.

"Well it's better than waiting around here to get eaten," said Susie. She started to climb outside.

"She's right," said Greg, following her. "Come on Lewis, get a move on!"

There was a crash against the door and Lewis saw the wood start to splinter. He clambered out of the window and teetered anxiously on the ledge.

16. A SPLASH IN THE POOL OF URD

Slowly, Lewis worked himself sideways after the other two.

"Hurry up, Lewis!" Greg urged.

"It's all right for you," Lewis complained. "With those magic shoes on you can't put a foot wrong."

There was a terrible crash as the door burst apart and with a roar the dragon bashed the flimsy barrier aside.

"Look, just keep close to the wall and you'll be fine," said Greg. "I won't let you fall."

The dragon's stone snout scraped through the window, but its head was too big to fit through. It gave a disgusted snort and ground its jaws in frustration. That was enough to speed Lewis along the ledge until he was pressed against Greg's side.

With a growl of frustration the dragon pulled back inside. One of the stone dwarfs crawled clumsily on to the ledge. As he drew himself upright he overbalanced and toppled to the ground. He hit the paving below with a resounding crash and shattered into a hundred pieces.

"Not exactly gymnasts, are they?" said Greg.

The other dwarfs bunched round the window and made a low moaning noise, as though shocked at the sight of their fallen comrade. None of them dared to follow.

Susie, Greg and Lewis continued to edge their way carefully around the corner of the palace. Above them the grey clouds were breaking up and a radiant sun blazed across the bright blue sky. From this height they could see out over the rooftops of Asgard.

The halls and palaces of the gods, which had looked ancient and derelict when they first arrived, now shone white and gold in the glorious sunlight, as if they had been newly built that day. Flashing banners of silver and green flew from the many towers, fluttering in the fresh breeze that was blowing across the city.

"Look!" said Susie pointing down. "There's some kind of a pond down there."

Below was a large circular pool of crystal clear water, the edge of which came right up to the palace wall. A memory jumped into Lewis' mind from when the ring had mapped out the whole of Asgard in his head.

"It's called the Pool of Urd," he said. "That's the House of the Norns on the other side and that's where they—"

"Forget the geography lesson!" Greg cut him off. "The point is we can jump from here and land in the water."

"Are you kidding?" said Lewis. "From this height?"

"This is nothing," said Susie. "Easy peasy."

"Maybe for you," Lewis protested.

"What's the big deal?" said Greg. "Last time we were at the Olympia pool in Dundee you jumped off a diving board this high."

"Only because you pushed me," Lewis snapped.

"Oh, right," said Greg, sneaking a hand round behind Lewis' back. "I remember now."

Without warning he gave his brother a shove that sent him tumbling through the air, his arms and legs flailing helplessly. Lewis hit the water with a squeal.

"Zero points for style," Greg commented drily.

"Let's see you do better," said Susie. She grabbed him by the shoulder and pitched him over the edge.

"Spinny!" Greg cried as he plummeted.

"Geronimo!" Susie yelled, jumping after him.

They splashed down a split second apart and bobbed up spitting out water.

"That was a dirty trick," Lewis spluttered as he floundered about.

"It worked, didn't it?" Greg countered.

He and Susie swam to the edge and hauled Lewis

out after them. Shaking the water from their hair and clothes, they set off down the nearest street, eager to put as much distance as they could between themselves and Odin's palace.

As they hurried along, the warm sunshine dried out their clothes and hair so quickly it was like they had never been wet at all. On either side of them the trees, which had been tired and wilting before, now stretched up tall and proud, sprouting fresh green leaves and stretching their mighty branches out against the sky.

Suddenly Susie pulled them all up short. "Hang on, where exactly are we going?" she demanded.

"Away from Loki," said Greg, pointing back at Odin's palace. "Unless you want to go a few more rounds with his armoured stooges."

"Yes, but where are we *going?*" Susie insisted. "We can't get home now that the Yggdrasil has fallen apart."

"She's right," said Lewis. "We can't just keep running. This is Loki's kingdom now. He's bound to catch up with us."

"Unless we can find some way to take him down," said Greg grimly. "We should make a fight of it at least. We've got Thor's hammer after all and I can move pretty fast in these shoes."

"I don't think that's much of a match for all the stuff Loki has in Odin's palace," said Lewis.

"Maybe we could drop by Thor's place and pick up a few thunderbolts to toss at him," Greg suggested.

"Thunderbolts are a meteorological phenomenon," Lewis informed him shortly. "They're not something you can throw around."

"Well, at least I had an idea," Greg retorted. "I don't hear you coming up with much."

"Greg does have a point," said Susie. "All sorts of gods – if you want to call them that – lived around here. Maybe one of them has something we can use."

"Thor told us that Surtur stole the treasures of Asgard and hid them on Earth," said Lewis. "That's why Thor's hammer was in our garage. There can't be much left behind."

Susie puffed out her cheeks and made an exasperated noise. "What about something that was nailed down or too big to move?" she said.

"A big cannon, for instance," said Greg. "You know, like Mons Meg in Edinburgh Castle."

"Vikings didn't have cannons," said Lewis, "and I'm pretty sure their gods didn't either."

"But if Asgard is powered up again," said Susie, gesturing at the city, "there must be *something* out there we can use."

Lewis felt a notion stirring at the back of his mind, telling him she was right. They had spotted something when they first arrived in Asgard, something that could help them.

He cast his thoughts back to the images of the city that the ring had sent spinning through his brain. There was the Avenue of Giants, the Palace of Wings, the Seven Wells, the Golden Market. A small voice seemed to whisper to him that somewhere in the city there was a way to defeat Loki, but the stream of images and facts swirled dizzyingly about him. He began to sway and both Greg and Susie grabbed hold to steady him.

"Take it easy, Lewis," said Greg. "I don't want you throwing up all over me."

"Something's coming to me," said Lewis. "There's a place we saw when we came into the city..."

"What?" Greg pressed him. "The wall? The gate?"

"Heimdall's Gatehouse!" Lewis exclaimed.

"Whose what?" said Greg.

"The place on the rock, remember?" said Susie. "With the horns."

Suddenly it was clear to Lewis, like a blurred picture coming into focus. "Heimdall was the guardian of the Bifrost, the Rainbow Bridge."

"How does that help us?" said Greg. "Thor said that bridge was smashed to bits."

"Yes, but a bridge that connects Asgard to Earth

can't be an ordinary bridge made of stone and steel," said Lewis. His thoughts were starting to connect now and with that he felt a glimmer of hope.

"You're right!" Susie enthused. "It would have to be an energy stream tunnelling through hyperspace."

"Yes, something like that," Lewis agreed.

"Hold on," said Greg, raising his hand. "Where is all this taking us?"

"Look," said Lewis, "if Loki can get Asgard back online, maybe we can restore the Bifrost as well. And if we can, Heimdall's Gatehouse would be the place to do it."

"We could go back to Earth and get help," said Susie.

"Sure," said Greg. "We could get the RAF to come and bomb Loki back to the stone age."

"Well, what are we standing around for?" said Susie. "Let's go!"

"Okay, it's this way," said Greg, setting off decisively.

Lewis grabbed him by the sleeve and pulled him back. "No," he said, pointing, "it's this way."

The layout of the city was still clear in his head from when he wore the ring. He was able to guide them swiftly down the tree-lined boulevards and wide avenues to the foot of the crag where Heimdall's gatehouse looked down on them.

As they arrived at the bottom of the path leading up

the slope, a horrid clanking made them turn and look down the broad street behind them.

"Not them again!" Lewis groaned.

A mob of bodiless armour, about twenty suits in all, Lewis estimated, was marching towards them, brandishing swords, axes and spears to show they meant business.

Greg caught Lewis by the elbow and pointed him toward the rock. "Lewis, you get up there," he told him. "Susie and I will hold them off while you fire up the beef roast."

"They don't look so tough," said Susie, taking a practice swing with the hammer. "Greg and I can handle this."

At a shove from Greg, Lewis started up the path.

"Let me have that rope of yours, Spinny," said Greg, unzipping her backpack and reaching inside. One eye on the approaching enemy, he formed one end of the rope into a loop.

"Pretty good lasso," Susie commented. "Where did you learn to do that?"

"Cowboy camp," said Greg.

Susie gave him a sceptical look. "Are you pulling my leg?"

"No, really, there's a place down in the Borders Dad took us to a couple of years ago. You get to wear big stetson hats and do all kinds of cowboy stuff."

While the other two prepared for battle, Lewis raced up the path to the top of the crag. It was a flat expanse of rock the size of a football pitch. In the centre was a marble building with a great iron door in the wall.

There was no sign of a lock or a handle. Lewis pushed at it, first on one side, then the other, but no matter how hard he pressed, the iron slab remained stubbornly shut. He ran his hands over it, searching for a button or a switch that might spring it open, but there was none.

Down below, a tide of living armour surged forward to engulf Greg and Susie. Susie greeted their arrival with a warlike whoop.

17. BIFROST IS ON THE MENU

The armoured ranks surged forward. Susie took a swing with Mjolnir and whacked the first warrior square on the shield. The power of Thor's hammer sent him staggering back into his companions, bringing the whole mob to a shuddering halt.

"You have to hit them in just the right spot," Susie told Greg. "It's like taking a penalty shot."

Her next swing knocked the helmet off another body of metal, then she smashed the legs out from under a third.

Though Greg had no weapon, he was able to dodge around the armoured warriors while they reeled under Susie's attack. The Shoes of Vidar allowed him to move nimbly but he still felt the sharp blades swishing past him too close for comfort. As he ducked and ran, he looped his lasso over the helmet of one and wound the coils of rope around the others, tangling their iron limbs.

"Nice going, Greg!" Susie cheered. "They're on the ropes now!"

Up above, Lewis ran a complete circuit around the gatehouse, but could find no way inside. What he did discover was a marble stairway leading to the roof, so he sprinted up to the top.

Above him the twin pillars soared thirty metres into the air, their ends tapering to a point as they curved in towards each other until they were almost touching. At the foot of the pillars was a lectern of white marble inlaid with seven jewels, each a different colour.

The green stone was an emerald, Lewis knew, the blue would be a sapphire, the red a ruby. He guessed the one that was burnt orange was a garnet, but he couldn't name the yellow one or any of the others. What did they represent? Maybe all he had to do was touch them to power up the Bifrost.

He brushed his palm up and down then back and forth across the gems, but nothing happened. "No, it wouldn't that simple," he muttered to himself. There had to be a start-up sequence, but what?

The crash of combat from below interrupted his thoughts.

"Any time you can kick start that thing would be good!" Greg shouted.

"Get your skates on, Lewis!" Susie chimed in between hammer blows.

Lewis rubbed his temples and tried to concentrate. "The sequence, the sequence," he murmured.

There were seven jewels ... and there were seven letters in the name Bifrost. Maybe that was it. He tapped the sapphire, blue for 'B'. Then he patted the indigo stone. None of these stones started with 'F' as far as he knew, so he tapped the unknown yellow one and carried on until he had touched all seven jewels.

Nothing happened.

Down below, Susie had forced the attacking warriors into a compact mass and Greg had managed to wind the rope completely around them.

"Right, Spinny, grab hold and help me pull," said Greg.

Susie dropped Mjolnir and took a grip on the rope. Together they yanked at it, pulling it tighter and tighter. Caught in the coils, the metal creatures were forced together. They flailed about trying to free themselves, but in their mindless efforts to break free, they were bashing each other with their weapons. A helmet was dashed off one, an arm chopped off another, and one by one the suits of armour broke down into useless heaps of metal.

Greg and Susie let go of the rope and stepped back, panting and red-faced from the battle.

"Look at that!" Greg exclaimed breathlessly. "We demolished them!"

"Ka-BOOM!" Susie whooped.

Their glee was cut short as an angry roar shook the air.

"Now what?" Greg groaned.

Riding towards them up the broad avenue was Loki, seated on the back of the stone dragon. He dismounted and tossed a lump of coal at the dragon, who caught it in his mouth and swallowed it with a burp.

Susie snatched up the hammer and gave him the dirtiest look she had ever given anyone in her life.

Loki eyed the scattered mess of scrap metal on the ground and raised an eyebrow. "This is quite a mess you hooligans have made."

"The battle's over, Larry" said Greg boldly, "but you're welcome to surrender."

"Junior, that was only round one," Loki drawled.

He snapped his fingers and immediately the scattered pieces of armour began to quiver and slide across the ground. As if being assembled by an invisible workforce, the boots, breastplates and gauntlets all clipped themselves back into place until the whole force was restored. With a clank they stood to attention, their weapons at the ready.

"Welcome to round two," Loki declared, waving his troops forward.

This time the armoured figures spread out and came at them in a disciplined charge. They were no longer a disorganised crowd, but a proper military unit, guided by Loki's will.

Greg swallowed hard and clapped a hand on Susie's shoulder. "Watch yourself, Spinny," he warned.

"End of the final period," said Susie through gritted teeth. "Money time!"

Up on the roof Lewis was startled by the sounds of renewed combat. He tried his best to ignore it and focus on the problem at hand. Spelling had nothing to do with it, he was sure, but the different colours of the jewels *had* to be a clue.

Then it came to him. The Bifrost was also known as the Rainbow Bridge, and these gems, he realised with dawning excitement, were all the colours of the rainbow. Maybe what he had to do was activate them in the order they would be seen in a rainbow.

But what was that?

His science teacher Mr Gillespie had once taught the class a sentence you could use to remember what order the colours of the rainbow appeared in. The noise from below reminded him that the words were about somebody fighting a battle.

Lewis tugged on his lip and rubbed his ear, both of which should help him remember. *Richard of York* did something. Yes, that was it!

Richard of York gave battle in vain. The first letter of each word gave you the right colour.

He reached out a finger and tapped the ruby. A light immediately appeared inside the gem. He touched the orange stone next and the same thing happened. Quickly he completed the sequence: yellow, green, blue, indigo and violet.

By the time all seven gems were glowing, the air around him tingled with gathering force, like the prelude to a thunderstorm. Multi-coloured sparks were dancing around the pillars like fireflies and the air crackled with magical energy.

Lewis threw up an arm to protect his eyes as a blaze of rainbow light erupted between the pillars. It shot across the sky and into the distance, forming a huge arc of shimmering cosmic power. He lowered his arm and gaped in awe at the rainbow bridge spanning the sky from end to end.

His wonder was cut short when a pair of steel gauntlets clamped on to his shoulders. Twisting about, he found himself face to helmet with one of Loki's metal guards. It lifted him up and carried him, feet dangling, down the steps to where Loki stood beaming in fiendish glee.

Greg and Susie were also in the grip of their armoured enemies. The hammer Mjolnir lay on the ground where it had been forced from Susie's hand.

Susie struggled against the iron arms that encircled her. "Good work, Lewis," she said through gritted teeth. "You did your best."

Greg kicked against his captor. "Sorry we couldn't hold them."

Loki squinted up at the shimmering rainbow light and frowned. "I'd better shut that thing down. Then I'll deal with the three of you permanently."

"Don't kid yourself," Greg blurted out. "There's no way you can get rid of us."

"Let's see if you still think that once the dragon is chewing on your bones," said Loki with a cold smile.

The dragon took a step forward and bared its granite teeth. Greg tried desperately to wrench free of the iron grip of his captors. He could see Lewis and Susie had turned pale at the prospect of being turned into dragon food.

"Well, guys," said Susie, her voice catching, "I guess we didn't make it to the penalty shootout."

Loki had only taken his first step towards the stairs when something stopped him in his tracks. It was Thor's hammer. All of a sudden Mjolnir began to vibrate furiously, giving off a low hum as it did so.

"Spinny, are you doing that?" Greg asked.

Susie shook her head, her eyes wide with astonishment. "It's got nothing to do with me."

Slowly the hammer rose into the air and rotated above their heads.

Lewis gulped. "I think something big is up."

With a snarl Loki leapt into the air and made a grab for the hammer, but Mjolnir rose up beyond his reach. Dropping back down on his feet, Loki shook his fist and spat, "Drat that hunk of scrap!"

Suddenly Mjolnir stopped spinning and flew into the sky like a rocket, shooting over the rainbow bridge to disappear from sight.

As he watched it disappear, seething with frustration, Loki lost concentration and his control over the armour weakened. Greg, Lewis and Susie felt the iron limbs that held them go slack.

Loki made a sudden move for the stairway.

"Stop him!" Lewis exclaimed, wriggling loose. "He's going to shut off the Bifrost!"

Greg shook off his metal captor and threw himself at Loki. He wrapped his arms around the god's legs and brought him down in a rugby tackle. Loki kicked loose and got to his feet, grabbing hold of Greg. He shook him with inhuman strength and hurled him through the air to slam against the wall of the gatehouse.

Slipping loose of the armoured guards, Susie grabbed a shield from one of them. She thrust it out in front of her and charged right at Loki, knocking him backwards, slamming the shield into him.

Digging in his heels, Loki struck back. He snatched the shield from her and struck her a mighty blow with the back of his hand. Susie went tumbling across the ground like she had been hit with a battering ram.

Lewis was horrified, but his anger at Loki drove him forward. He rushed at the god, but reeled back when Loki flung a bolt of fire that exploded at his feet.

"That does it!" Loki screeched. "I'm going to barbecue the three of you right now!" He raised a menacing hand and fire flared from his fingertips. The flames moulded themselves into a roaring fireball, spitting and snapping.

But before the enraged god could let fly, a deep voice thundered out, "Loki, I say thee nay!"

The fireball sputtered out and Loki gazed up with a queasy expression on his thin face. Greg and Susie helped each other up and joined Lewis in gaping at an astonishing sight.

Descending from the sky on the rainbow bridge was a crowd of shining figures. The youngsters recognised Thor, though he looked taller now and held Mjolnir in his upraised hand. He was the one who had spoken, but his voice now had power and authority behind it.

The gods of Asgard arrived on the roof of the gatehouse and strode down the steps in a stately procession. There was a glorious vigour about them, as if they had woken from a long sleep into the sunshine of a better day.

Lewis didn't need a magic ring to tell him who they were. He recognised them from the Norse legends he had been reading ever since their first encounter with Loki.

At the head of the procession was a tall, white-bearded man with a patch over one eye and a pair of ravens sitting on his shoulders. This was Odin, the king of the gods. Beside him walked his queen, Frigga, with her silver hair and crown of gold.

Close behind them was Thor and the one-handed god Tyr, clutching a flashing sword. Clothed in white with a face that shone like the sun was Balder. Freya, the goddess of love, came next, wearing a green robe entwined with ivy and bluebells.

Lewis estimated that there had to be at least a hundred of them. Many of them stayed on the roof to observe as Odin advanced on the god of mischief and magic.

Loki seemed to shrink before them. He took a fearful step back and forced a weak grin.

"Guys," he said brightly, "good to see you. Look, I've smartened the place up for you." He made an expansive gesture at the city. "It'll be like you've never been gone. Tell you what, the drinks are on me."

"Silence, Loki!" Odin commanded in a voice like the crash of a waterfall. He waved his hand and Loki was enveloped in swirling bands of golden light that bound his arms to his sides. More bands of light encircled his legs and he fell to the ground, muttering curses.

"I will brook no more of your foul utterances," said Odin, and wound a shining gag around Loki's mouth.

"It's about time somebody shut him up," Greg commented under his breath.

The king of the gods looked out over the city and nodded slowly. "It is good to be back in the realm eternal," he said. "And it is thanks to these children." He bent a friendly gaze on Greg, Lewis and Susie.

"It's the Bifrost, isn't it," said Lewis. "Once Asgard was linked to Earth again, you all got your god powers back."

"That's right, Lewis," said Thor. "And the treasures returned to their rightful owners." He gave Mjolnir a contented pat.

"That all happened pretty fast," said Greg.

"Down in your earthly lands of Midgard time passes more swiftly than it does here in Asgard," Odin explained. "Here time can flow in any direction I choose."

"Sure, it's some kind of a space–time warp, isn't it?" said Susie.

"We just call it magic," said Thor with a shrug.

"My son Thor spoke truly of you children," Odin declared approvingly. "You are indeed worthy to be warriors of Asgard, Lewis the Wise, Greg the Bold and Susie the Brave. You shall join us in a feast to celebrate your courage and your victory."

"If it's all the same to you," said Susie, "can we go home now? I've got a week booked at hockey camp. And my folks will be worried about me."

"Ours too," said Lewis.

Odin smiled. "I already told you, Lewis, that I can bend time itself to my will. I will return you to Earth before your kinsfolk even know you are gone."

"What about this guy?" asked Greg, jerking a thumb at Loki who was wriggling helplessly on the ground.

"I have a place of exile waiting for him," said Odin, "beyond the bounds of space and time. He will not trouble your world again."

Susie stood over the fallen god of magic and beamed a smile of victory. "You see," she said, "I warned you. This is what you get for calling me *toots!*"

18. WHO IS LARRY O'KEEFE?

The journey back to Earth along the Bifrost took only a few seconds. Heimdall, the guardian of the rainbow bridge, adjusted the controls and waved them forward.

The moment Greg, Lewis and Susie set foot upon the arc of light, they found themselves hurtling forward with stars, planets and glowing clouds whooshing past them. It all melted into a blur then there they were, standing on the summit of Hallowhill.

"Phew, that was some trip!" Greg exclaimed.

"Hyperspace," said Susie, trying to sound casual. "It's the only way to travel."

Lewis shook off his dizziness and gazed about him. The hilltop looked perfectly normal, as if a cosmic tree had never taken root there. A short way off, a lady was throwing a stick for her spaniel to chase, while down below the Kinnessburn was rushing by, still swollen with the melted snow from Loki's supernatural winter.

"I don't know if it's the trip or all that roast boar,"

said Lewis, rubbing his tummy, "but I don't feel so good."

"That was the mead," Greg laughed. "It's like beer. I warned you not to drink so much of it."

"Oh, it was dead tasty," said Susie, smacking her lips. "And what about these?" She raised her right hand to admire the gold ring on her finger, which was decorated with a lightning bolt. They all had one, a gift from Odin.

"These rings are a mark of the favour of Asgard," the king of the gods had told them, "an honour bestowed upon only a few."

"What do you think they do?" Susie wondered, tilting her hand so that the gold gleamed in the bright morning sunshine.

"Let's not find out," Lewis advised. "The safest thing would be to lock them in a lead box and bury them in a really deep hole."

"What are you so scared of, Lewis?" Greg scoffed. "I bet they do something really cool."

"Haven't you had enough of Asgardian magic?" said Lewis. "We're lucky to be alive as it is."

Susie rubbed her ring with a fingertip. "Well, it's not doing anything so far."

"Stop messing about with it," Lewis pleaded. "You might start a thunderstorm or something worse."

"Come on," said Greg. "We'd better get back to the house and see what's happening."

They headed down the hill and strolled along Rivermill Gardens to the Spinetti house. As they approached the front door Mr McBride came out with his pipe in his hand. "Oh there you are," he said. "We wondered what had happened to you three."

"We nipped out for an early stroll," said Susie. "You know, seeing as how the weather's turned out so nice."

"You haven't seen Sven, have you?" Dad asked, stuffing some tobacco into the bowl of his pipe. "He dashed off shouting something about a beef roast. It looked like his leg had healed up overnight."

"We passed him on the way back," said Lewis.

"He had to get back to SAPS HQ and report to his boss, the king of Scandivaria," said Greg.

"Can we go home now, Dad?" Lewis yawned. "I think I'm needing my bed."

"Really?" said his dad. "But you only just got up?"

"We've packed a lot in," said Greg.

Dad lit his pipe and took a puff. "Well, I got that handyman McGregor on the phone. He says he'll have our house fixed up in a jiffy, so you might as well pack up your stuff."

At that moment Garth Makepeace swept out of

the door with a phone pressed to his right ear. He had a mug of coffee in his other hand and slurped on it as he talked. "That's right," he was saying, "make sure everybody's there, Steve, George, Jerry, the whole gang. They'll all want to be in on it."

He flicked off the call, dropped the phone in his pocket, and took a last swig of coffee. "Thanks for everything, Al," he said, handing Mr McBride the empty mug. "It's been a ball."

"Is this you going, Garth?" asked Susie. She couldn't hide her disappointment.

"Got to fly," said Makepeace. "I'm going to turn all this crazy stuff we went through into the greatest movie ever. Get this title," he enthused. *"Iceblast: Battle For The Frozen Earth*. Cool, huh? We set it in New York and I play Jack Breaker, an Arctic survival expert. I fight my way through the snow to rescue my gorgeous girlfriend who's being held prisoner in the Empire State Building, which has been turned into a giant icicle."

"Sounds pretty good," said Greg.

"Good?" said Makepeace. "It'll be a monster! But only if I can catch my plane on time to sign the deal."

As he spoke a taxi pulled up and the driver got out looking astonished. "You really are him!" he gasped. *"Him!"*

"Did you think it was a prank call?" said Makepeace. "There's an extra hundred in it for you if you get me to the airport by noon. Oh, and pull in at an ATM on the way."

"A what?"

"A cash machine," Lewis translated.

"Of course," said the driver, opening the back door of the cab. "Of course, Mr... Mr..." He gave everybody a wide-eyed look. "It's *HIM!*"

"You kids stay in touch," said Makepeace, slipping into the taxi. "I'll fly you over for the movie premiere." He whipped out his phone and clamped it to his ear as the driver got into the front seat.

As the taxi pulled away everybody waved and Greg called out, "Make sure you do your own stunts!"

"I bet he'll want me to be in that film," said Mr McBride with a chuckle. "You know, a wee cameo role."

"I wonder who'll play Larry O'Keefe," said Lewis.

Mum appeared in the doorway. "Who exactly is this Larry O'Keefe I keep hearing you talk about?" she asked.

"Nobody, Mum," said Lewis.

"Yeah, you can forget all about him, Mrs Mac," said Susie. "He got what was coming to him."

As they filed inside Mum noticed their rings. "They're

impressive pieces of jewellery," she said. "Where did they come from?"

"Sven gave them to us," said Susie, showing off her ring.

"To thank us for helping with his investigation," Lewis added.

"It means we're honorary SAPS," said Greg. "Cool, eh?"

"Have you had any breakfast yet?" Mum asked. "There's bacon and eggs in the kitchen."

"I couldn't eat a thing," Lewis groaned.

"Me neither," said Susie. "Well, maybe a slice of toast, if there's any going."

"I think we can manage that," said Mum, heading for the kitchen. Susie followed her while Greg and Lewis went to their room and bundled up their pyjamas and sleeping bags.

As they headed out the front door Susie was waiting there, munching on a piece of buttered toast.

"Of course the great thing about *gods*," she said, twiddling her ring, "is that they have really good manners. They always thank people who've helped them."

"Yes, yes," said Lewis. "Thanks. We're really grateful to you for everything. Really."

Susie munched down the last of her toast and

directed a hard stare at Greg. "Greg, I'm off to hockey camp for a week," she said. "Isn't there anything you want to say to me before I go?"

"Well, right, Susie, it's like Lewis said," Greg agreed, shuffling his feet. "I mean, we couldn't have done it without you, you know. So thanks."

"There's no need to be so shy, Greg," said Susie firmly. "You can kiss me if you want to."

"Kiss you!" Greg was appalled.

As he stood there, aghast, Susie swooped in and planted a buttery kiss right on his lips.

"There," she said, drawing back with a grin. "That's that done at last."

Greg's face turned bright red and he wiped a hand across his mouth. "Spinny, I've told you already, I am not your boyfriend."

Susie laughed and punched him painfully on the arm.

Greg was still rubbing the bruise as he and Lewis walked down Bannock Street towards home.

"Of course, the worst thing about this is that we can't tell anybody," he said. "Nobody will know what happened."

"Probably just as well," said Lewis. "I don't even want to think about how close Loki came to blowing up the whole world."

"Don't worry about it," said Greg. "If he shows up again, remember I still have my secret weapon."

"What's that?" asked Lewis with a frown.

Greg flashed him a grin. "Awesomeness."

Lewis laughed in spite of himself and followed him into the house.